Fugitive

Curse of the Hybrids
Book 5

LISA LAGALY

PUBLISHING

Published in the United States of America

First Printing, 2025

ISBN
ebook: 978-1-966455-12-7
paperback: 978-1-966455-13-4

LL Publishing
Lisal.author@gmail.com

Previously

After being kidnapped by a hired thug at the end of her second semester of college, Honey escaped her parents' murderer, Gaian Graves, with the help of her grandmother, Rachel Wixx. Her grandmother gave her a charm so that witches wouldn't be able to feel her wolf side and drove her to London, Canada to a witch-only boarding school. Gaian, under the guise of finding the missing Wixx heir, but in reality seeking revenge on Honey's mother for choosing a wolf over him, and because no fifteen-year-old hybrid brat was going to get the best of him, kept searching for her. After several months and no sign of Honey among the wolves, he put out a general call to all witches asking for information. Honey was warned in time to escape, but instead of disappearing again, she opted to apply her new magical know-how to a century-old curse on the land her cousin, a new alpha, needed for his pack. She succeeded but Gaian learned of her whereabouts. One of Honey's friends, Alpha-to-be Brayton Mooney caught Gaian spying on the pack and confronted him. Honey arrived just in time to save Brayton's life, but not in time to prevent him from being severely burned. She bound Gaian's powers so he could never burn anyone again, but with his arrest by the Enforcers, it won't be long before the whole world knows she exists.

1

BRAYTON – JULY 18 – INDIANA

"Turn it up."

"Yes, Your Highness. Will there be anything else Your Highness?" Cici asked, bowing beside the big screen TV his mom had ordered hung in his room while he was in the hospital.

Brayton threw a pillow. Cici easily dodged it. Two weeks of taking it easy and he was already losing his skills.

"Why are we watching this again?" Malcolm asked, tilting precariously back in his chair and tossing pieces of Brayton's chocolate drizzled caramel popcorn into his mouth.

"Because Nathan and Walter are making a presentation, doofus," Cici said, plopping down on the side of the bed. "It's not everyday people our age are allowed to appear in front of the council."

"Over-achievers." The next piece of popcorn flew over Malcolm's head and bounced off the wall and into his hair.

"Stop it, Malcolm. If you make a mess Mom's going to blame me."

"No she won't," Cici said. "She'd never blame her precious, blind Brayton."

"I'm not blind."

"Shh. There they are," Rhys hissed from his chair on the other side of the bed.

"They're on?" Mom asked from the doorway. "Malcolm, stop leaning back in the chair. Do you know how much I paid for that?"

"Yes, Luna."

Malcolm let the chair drop to four legs then leaned forward and chortled, "Oh My Go...osh, did they just introduce Walter as Beta of the Honey Pack?"

"They did," Brayton smiled to himself.

Half his face felt stiff and might always feel that way, but at least he had a mouth to smile with. The healers the witch council had finally sent had done a great job considering how bad it had been. Except for the eye patch and the missing hair which would hopefully grow back, Cici assured him he didn't look odd at all.

Mom was shaking her head. "Those boys will regret naming their pack after her. Something horrible is going to happen to all those lovely women and children."

"Stop it, Mom. It wasn't Honey's fault and it wasn't yours. It was mine. I shouldn't have confronted that witch without back-up." And he should have worn the charm Honey gave him, but saying it again would just set Mom off.

"There wouldn't have been a witch and you wouldn't have even been in Yellowstone if it weren't for Honey."

And Zavier would be dead and who knows what would have happened to him but arguing with her was useless. He turned his attention back to the TV where Nathan had begun presenting their plea that the law requiring immediate death of a hybrid be changed to allow for testing first to ensure the child didn't have powers that

5

would negate the curse. They wisely, he thought, didn't mention Honey. Instead, Nathan pointed out that there was a clear correlation between the disappearance of certain magical powers, such as the ability to break curses, and institution of the law.

"*Do you have any evidence to support your claims?*" a witch asked.

"*How can we have evidence if all the babies have been killed?*" Nathan responded. "*Changing the law to allow for testing will not harm anyone and may even prevent unnecessary deaths.*"

"*It is well documented that hybrids are monsters. Witches and wolves are genetically incompatible,*" the witch claimed.

"*Actually, witches and wolves are the same species,*" Walter said. "*They even have the same number of chromosomes. It's not the genes that are the problem, it is the curse. I have a copy of a peer-reviewed scientific journal that goes into more depth if you're interested.*" He held up several papers stapled together.

"*What journal,*" the woman snapped.

"*Journal of Magical Genetics.*"

"*Probably a copy-cat site,*" the woman sniffed.

A man stood and stepped up regally next to Walter. "*I assure you, it is real.*"

"Oh, wow, now that is a beautiful British accent," Cici sighed.

"Who is he?" Brayton's mom asked at the same time the woman on the screen did.

"*I am Dr. Thaddeus Wallace, head of the Department of Genetics at Greens University and the lead author of the paper. When I heard what Nathan and Beta Walter were attempting, I volunteered to stand with them. I thought it high time someone addressed the horribly incorrect 'facts' that everyone quotes as true.*"

"Wow, they found a big gun," Rhys said under his breath.

"Have you heard of him?" Cici asked.

"Yeah. He's the author of one of the books I'll be using next semester."

"You already bought your books?" Malcolm gaped.

"I got some at the end of the semester. One of the guys down the hall was selling his."

"Quiet," Brayton demanded. "Who's that woman who just joined them?"

"*I'm Naomi Davis, Mg.D.*," the woman who had just appeared on screen said.

"Mg.D.," Malcolm asked. "What's that?"

"Doctor of Magic," Mom answered. "Listen."

"*You asked if it is possible to test for the curse. I believe so. I have examined samples pre- and post- curse and I believe I have developed a test that can distinguish between those that are cursed and those that are not. The problem, of course, is that I have no way to verify my findings because there's no way to follow the lives of the negative samples because they never get a chance to live them.*"

"*What about people who are cursed through association? Will it identify them?*" someone asked.

"*Again, all the samples I've been able to acquire are post-extermination, so I cannot say for sure, but if there's someone out there who would like to be tested pre-extermination, please contact me. I'm on Facebook.*"

Brayton glanced at his mom. She turned toward him at the same time, with wide eyes. "We should get you tested."

"Why?"

"You'd make the perfect test subject. She could take before and after samples."

"After what?"

Her eyes dropped. "Well, after Honey is, you know."

"Mom, for the last time, Honey is not cursed!"

"Your dad and I should be tested too," she mumbled. "I mean, we didn't know until she was out of our control, but we harbored the monster. I'd turn her in if I could. The curse has to know that."

"Mom, Honey is not a monster."

Mom looked at him with her eyes full of tears. "Oh Brayton, I'm so sorry I failed you. I was just trying to make the world a better place."

"Stop it, Mom. You didn't fail anyone."

Why did he even bother saying it? She never listened.

"Shh, there's your father."

The camera had panned over to where all the alphas were sitting. To even be considered for the vote, at least one alpha and one witch had to make the motion to vote for it, then there might be weeks of arguing over the wording before the vote was finally called.

His dad stood. Oh no. Dad was going to shoot them down before the council even got started. He supported Mom. He always did.

"I'm Alpha Brandon Mooney from Indiana. I propose we put the amendment to the vote right now as written, with one small addition – that if the curse is not evident either physically or magically, then the lives of the child and their parents will be spared. I know some of you will argue we need evidence that the test will work before we vote on anything, but I think it's abundantly clear in most cases which children are cursed. It's the others we're trying to save. I have met one of these exceptions. She's beautiful, brilliant, strong, and has a heart of gold. She's saved my son's life more than once. I didn't know what she was until about a week ago and I don't

know where she is now, but to kill her simply due to something she had no control over would be an absolute waste."

There was a brief moment when everyone in the court was absolutely silent, then they all started yelling at once. The witch in charge of the meeting lifted her gavel, then set it down with a shake of her head.

"Damn that man. Why wouldn't he listen to me? He's cursed everyone," Brayton's mom said.

"We aren't cursed Mom!" Brayton yelled.

A loud boom went off on the screen. The camera panned to a male witch who was blowing on his finger like it was a gun. He pointed to the witch in charge with a grin.

"*Thank you. Now that I have your attention. Alpha Mooney, that's quite a confession. Who is this wunderkind?*"

"*Before I give you her name, I'd like to assure everyone that you are not cursed. I asked Dr. Davis to test me and several other people in the audience before I made my announcement. She will test them again in front of you.*"

"*But there's no way to show her test works!*" someone yelled.

"*She has been provided with a sample from the child I mentioned,*" Brayton's dad said.

"*But you said you don't know where she is.*"

"*I do not, but she knows where she is and she found a way to mail the…someone a sample of her blood. Dr. Davis, if you would please?*"

"*Who is in contact with her?*" someone asked.

Dr. Davis started speaking before anyone could answer.

"*Thanks Alpha Mooney,*" she said in a normal tone, then under her breath mumbled, "*although a little warning that I was about to try out my experimental device in front of the whole world would have been nice,*" likely forgetting half the audience was composed of super-hearing wolves. She stepped out into the middle of the room carrying a plastic box with a snap-on lid. Two attendants rushed forward with a small wooden table and placed it before her in the exact center of the room. She opened her box and started laying the contents on the table. *"First, all those of you who provided samples earlier, please step forward."*

She explained how her test worked while she jabbed their fingers. The test was basically a small piece of paper with three dots: one for the positive control, one for the negative, and one for the test sample. To read it, you compared the colored rings that formed around the drops of blood you put in each spot. Cursed rings were black whereas non-cursed rings were a very light gray. The positive, cursed control was from a cursed fetus. The negative, uncursed control was from a normal baby who could not have any knowledge of a cursed person.

"Now, there's something odd with Alpha Mooney's sample. His rings are white. I've often suspected that part of the reason my negative controls give a signal is because we're all cursed, but at a low level. If Alpha Mooney has had contact with this child and she is, in fact, a curse breaker, it would explain the lack of color."

"Curse breaker? Who said anything about her being a curse breaker?" someone in the audience yelled.

Dr. Davis blinked up at the speaker as if her statement hadn't been profound at all. *"Logically, she'd have to be."*

The witches started murmuring among themselves so loudly it sounded like a hive of bees.

His dad was the third one in line to be tested. The camera zoomed in on his father's test which was displayed with all the other tests on a big screen at the front of the council chamber. It ended up looking exactly the same as the first one. The camera panned out. None of the new tests looked any different from the older ones.

After she'd gone through the whole line, Dr. Davis held up a clear vial full of red liquid. "*Here's the child's sample. Let's see what happens.*"

Brayton discreetly wiped a tear from his good eye. He was crying over blood for Pete's sake.

Honey's blood seemed to sparkle just before it soaked into the test spot. No gray appeared, just like he'd known it wouldn't, then the light gray of the positive sample and the black of the negative sample started to disappear.

"*Amazing,*" Dr. Davis breathed.

Brayton wasn't sure if she meant for that to be heard or not.

"*How do we know that wasn't a trick?*" someone yelled.

"*Or that your test isn't backwards?*" someone added.

"*That's what the controls are for,*" Dr. Davis said calmly.

"*Let me test the blood,*" an older woman dressed in clothes that looked like they were from the 1800s and with the hair to match demanded. No one stopped her when she rose from her seat in the witch's section and marched down the steps.

"Who is that?" Cici asked. "Someone needs to tell her it's time to update her wardrobe."

"She sounds southern," Rhys commented.

"You would know," Malcolm teased.

Rhys did have a thing for southern women.

The witch had reached the table. From a small, beaded bag, she pulled two items, one that looked like an extra-large guitar pick and a one that looked like a CD. "*Test for origins,*" she said, holding up the guitar pick, then setting it

11

firmly on the table, "*and a test for powers.*" She sat the disk next to the pick.

The camera zoomed in again as Dr. Davis put a little blood on the tip of the pick and the center of the CD.

"*I can tell you her bloodline,*" a woman's voice declared from somewhere near the top of the chamber. The camera view split to show the test and a short, plump, grand-motherly looking woman holding her head up proudly. "*She is a Wixx. She is my granddaughter and wherever you are dear, know that I am immensely proud of you.*"

"*You knew about her Rachel?*" the head witch asked.

"*Only for the last few months. She's why Madeline disappeared. My daughter was hiding her, raising her, with the help of her chosen husband, a wolf. She chose a lot better than we did. Her intended turned out to be a murderer.*"

An even older lady stood up in the midst of the witches and glared at the first. "*Sit down Rachel!*"

"*I will when I am done, Mother. My granddaughter is not cursed. She is perfect and she is beautiful both as a witch and in her wolf form.*"

"That ancient lady is Honey's Great-grandmother? She's scary," Malcolm commented.

"*I have a message from my granddaughter,*" Honey's Grandmother said, unfolding a piece of notebook paper.

"*You've seen her recently?*" the head witch snapped.

Rachel Wixx frowned at the head witch, but unlike her mother, Rachel Wixx didn't look scary at all. "*Of course not. She knows how to mail a letter.*" Rachel pushed up her glasses and read. "*She says the original curse was made by the witches of the five ruling families after one of the great plagues. They each have a copy written on something metal. One of our Wixx ancestors melted ours down years ago. She wants to encourage the rest of you:*

the Lamberts, the Brights, the Evelstones, and the family for which she doesn't know the name, to destroy your copies. Enough people have died and suffered due to the curse. You don't need a law and you don't need a curse breaker. You only need to destroy the curse."

"But that would mean…" a witch started.

"She also says we are in the twenty-first century and it's time we evolve beyond our medieval mindset. Magical prejudice is just as disgusting as prejudice due to skin color or national origin or religion. Being friends with a wolf or witch doesn't mean you have to marry them."

"That sounds like something she would say," Cici said.

Brayton lifted his eye patch and discretely wiped the moisture out from under it. Honey was putting up a good fight without being present. He was so proud of her.

"The tests are complete," the 1800's woman announced. *"Wixx and wolf as Rachel Wixx stated. The girl has powers of necromancy and evocation, so clearly not a curse breaker."*

Rachel Wixx was shaking her head and by the way her lips were moving was saying 'that's not right', but no one could hear her over the noise in the chamber.

"Necromancy? Doesn't that mean she can raise the dead?" Malcolm asked.

"That witch is lying," Brayton said. "Honey makes shields."

"You don't know that for sure," Mom said. "She only gave you that charm. She didn't say she made them, and she did speak to a dead woman. We really don't know anything about her."

Half the alphas were standing, trying to get the attention of the witch in charge. Another bang went off, but it didn't have the same effect as before. The woman in charge banged her gavel a few times, trying to get everyone's attention, then finally gave up and pointed it at the first standing wolf. "*Speak.*"

"*The witch lies. We can smell it,*" he stated loudly.

"*Do you all concur?*"

Brayton relaxed as every single wolf nodded.

The woman in charge shook her head. "*Filia, you should have known they'd smell right through that. What's the correct result?*"

"*Hmph,*" the woman said, lifting her nose in the air. "*You can't blame a witch for trying to keep the rest of you from blindly following where the wolves are leading us.*"

Cici pointed at the screen. "Look, the labels are changing."

"Big whoop. I still can't read them," Malcolm complained.

"*Abjuration and transmutation,*" Rachel Wixx announced from where she was still standing. "*Transmutation allows her to become a wolf and abjuration gives her the ability to protect from and break spells. It is clear evidence she could be the curse breaker the doctor claims.*"

"*Thank you, Rachel,*" the woman in charge said, "*but as we all know, all the witches that is, there are many smaller branches to each of the main branches of magic. She could simply be a maker of shields, for example. In any event, we have gotten quite far off topic. The question before the council is whether to amend the law to allow for testing and to spare the lives of those that do not appear to be cursed. Are there any others who would like to speak or present evidence for or against this motion?*"

Half the council raised their hands.

"This is going to take a while. Brayton, you should take a nap," his mom said.

"Mom, I'm fine. I'm healed."

"You are not healed. You will never be healed."

"Mom."

"I'm going to go make more of that popcorn," she sniffed.

"Mom."

Malcolm put his hand out so that it was in Brayton's face. "Don't stop her. That stuff is good."

"Wanna go to the gym while they debate, Brayton," Cici asked. "We can watch it down there."

"Sure. You guys go ahead. I'll be down in a few."

Cici gave him a sympathetic look before she scooted off the bed. Yeah, it took him a little longer to get dressed because everything was stiff, but it was getting better. The magical cream one of the healers had given him was slowly loosening up the skin that his healing powers had produced so quickly. That wasn't the reason he'd asked for more time though.

He grabbed some clothes after Rhys and Malcolm left and headed for the bathroom. He doubted Mom was spying on him with that little camera at the top of the big screen, but he wasn't going to take chances. Inside the bathroom he put his work-out clothes on the toilet seat, made sure the door was locked, then reached into the far back corner of the bathroom cabinet where even his mother didn't clean. The 'magic slate' with the big green happy face that Liam had snuck in to him while he was in the hospital was right where he'd left it. He really should fix that eye patch he'd scribbled over one eye in one of his lower moments.

Hey H, you there? he wrote. Liam had said she was almost exactly 12 hours ahead of their time, which could

15

mean she was in Kazakhstan, India, or one of the small countries around it according to Google.

He couldn't help the smile that rose when words appeared in Honey's loopy handwriting. *I am.*

Are you watching?

No signal, but Luca is recording it.

Your grandmother was amazing.

She was there?

Yeah, so was your great-gma. She was scary.

Yep.

My dad spoke up for you.

He did? But I thought your mom thinks I'm cursed.

I'm sure he will get an ear-full when he gets home.

Tell him thanks for me.

I will. Did you find a college to go to there?

There's not really one close, besides there's a lot to look at.

You be careful. With your luck you'd trip over a pot and wake an evil genie.

Who told you about that?

He swore his heart stopped for a moment, then he realized she had to be joking. There were no such things as genies. *Ha. Ha.*

:)

You forgot the eye patch.

You're the one with the eye patch, not me. It's a very nice eye patch though. Dr. Ziga sent me a picture.

Just of the eye patch?

A picture of a toothy happy face with an eye patch appeared.

Is that supposed to be me?

I never claimed to be an artist.

Smart move. I better go. Everyone is waiting for me in the gym. Same time-ish tomorrow?

Yeah.

Night, H

Night, BB.

What does BB mean? He asked for the umpteenth time. Again, no answer, darn her.

2

HONEY - JULY 21 - NEPAL

Somewhere, a rooster crowed. The braying donkey sounded a lot closer. He was probably on the porch again, right under her window. The rain had already started, or perhaps it had never stopped. Honey stretched and stood to look out the window. Despite the low-hanging clouds, the mountains were beautiful and green, but also extremely muddy. She normally didn't mind mud, but after weeks of wading through it to plant baby rice plants, she was ready for something else.

The colorful curtain hung over the doorway shifted to the side. "Good Morning, Honey," Dr. Ziga's sister, Divya, said from the doorway, "Are you ready for more planting?"

Honey groaned. Divya laughed.

"We are near done. If we start early, this may be the last day. Then we can par-ty." She swayed her hips so that her colorful skirt swished around her ankles. "Full moon tonight."

"Really?" Honey had completely lost track of the days and the moon thanks to the continual cloud cover.

Divya laughed. "I know, it's hard to tell, right. It's still there though, I promise."

"Ama, Ama, Ama!"

"Oof," Divya said when one of her children ran into her at full speed and threw her little arms around her legs.

"Shanti threw a chicken at me."

Divya shook her finger at the boy chasing the little girl. "Now Shanti, I told you, no chickens in the house," she grinned, "unless you're cooking one. I just had the best idea. You could pluck a chicken for the meal tonight."

The boy quickly backed away waving his hands, palms up. "No, no, Ama." He cupped a hand around his ear. "Oh, listen, is that Buwa? I should see."

Divya laughed as he ran off. "Such an actor." She hugged the girl still clinging to her. "You are safe from chickens now, little one. Go see if Auntie Pari needs any help with the baby." Divya gave a satisfied sigh when her daughter obediently went the opposite direction of her brother. "I better go make sure there's some breakfast left for you. You should brush your hair."

"Thanks," Honey said with more than a touch of sarcasm. Her curls and the constant humidity had become a source of amusement for everyone but herself. Divya laughed again.

Honey waited until Divya's footsteps had faded away before stretching out her fourth finger and pulling her backpack out of the nether. Not for the first time, she wondered if Divya had noticed she wasn't using the furniture she'd been provided to store her things, but she was pretty sure the woman wasn't a snooper. Like her brother, Divya was a wolf and super nice. She had accepted Dr. Ziga's hastily scrawled explanation – that Honey was a college student who wanted to do something a little different for summer break – without question despite Honey's abrupt appearance via portal.

From the top of the main compartment of her backpack, she pulled out her brush and the three magic slates she now carried with her: one for Brayton, one for the guys, and one for Frederica. Frederica had surprised her with a pair for them when Honey had asked her to buy a set from her cousin so she could communicate with Brayton. Frederica's slate had a unicorn. Honey had drawn an eye patch on the green face on Brayton's slate to keep it straight from the guys' slate and because him smiling with an eye patch was much better than what she saw in her dreams.

Brayton didn't usually write to her until evening, his time, but this morning his slate was covered in writing.

Enforcers came today. Searched for you. Mom compliant. Dad watchful. Grandpa pissed. Found cameras, microphones after they left. Probably more. They also searched for magical stuff. Luckily didn't find this. I warned Littles. Still no vote. Some want to leave as is, some want to amend the law, and some want to destroy curse and law. Everyone wants Honey. Stay safe.

The boy's slate simply said, in Luca's handwriting: *Anthill stirred. <u>Do not</u> add Honey.*

Frederica on the other hand, sounded completely oblivious. *Can I come over? (sent 6:05 pm)*

Honey should probably say no, but after all her help, she trusted Frederica. Plus, as far as she could tell, she was Frederica's only close friend. *Sure, as long as you're not followed (sent 6:30 am).*

Almost immediately, her message disappeared and the wall in front of her started wavering. Frederica popped out of her portal with a grin and…

"What are you wearing?" spilled out of Honey's mouth.

Frederica spun around, making the multiple layers of pink tulle on her skirt fly out. "Do you like it?"

"It's very pink."

Frederica laughed. "It's my dress for my cousin's wedding."

"Does the crown go with it?"

Frederica touched the circlet of stars sitting on top of her blond hair. "Yes. She's having a fairy tale reception and…"

"You're a fairy."

"Yep."

"Looks good. All you need are some wings."

"I know," Frederica huffed, "but my sister said only the bridesmaids get wings."

"Let me guess, she's a bridesmaid."

"Yep."

"You should take a pair in case she's wrong."

"Good idea. Oh." Frederica put her hand to her head and stumbled forward.

Honey jumped to her feet and caught her before she fell.

"I've never portalled twelve hours away before, just three," she said while Honey helped her sit on the bed.

"Lay down and rest for a while. You want some food?"

"I just ate."

"Well, lay down then. Don't forget to take off your crown."

"Good idea."

Honey grabbed her things before Frederica crashed on top of them, then moved to the front of the mirror to make her daily attempt to control her hair.

"Hey, did the enforcers visit your house?"

"No," Frederica said groggily. "Why?"

"They're looking for me."

"I know. You're on the news. It's a good picture."

"Great."

"Yeah, my pictures never turn out that good."

"Get some sleep. I'll be back in a few minutes."

"Wait, I came to ask you if you would be my guest."

Honey blinked at her over her shoulder. "You just said everyone is looking for me."

"You can wear a disguise. You'd make a great elf, like one of those ones with a sword."

"I don't know how to use a sword."

"Or a bow."

"I don't know how to do that either."

"They'd be plastic anyway."

"Would I get pointy ears?"

"Oh, yes," Frederica said eagerly, perking up even though Honey could tell she'd drained herself.

"Nap first, then we'll talk."

Silly girl. It was hard to believe Frederica was only a few months younger than her. Honey felt like she was years older.

Frederica was still asleep when Honey checked on her after planting rice most of the day, and later half-way through the party. Honey was surprised Frederica's father hadn't come looking for her, but perhaps he thought she was sleeping in her own bed. By 8 pm (8 am London,

Canada time), she knew it wouldn't be smart to let her sleep any further.

"Frederica wake up."

Frederica pulled the blanket she'd crawled under at some point over her head. "Go away Mom."

"I am not your mother."

A hand came out to swat at Honey. "Go away Victoria."

"Really? You think I'm Victoria?"

The blanket came down and Frederica looked up at her with wide eyes. "Honey!"

"What is that beeping noise?"

"Dad, made me a portal communicator." Frederica dug under the covers and pulled out an oval device slightly smaller than a cell phone and pressed on it. "Yeah Dad."

"If you're with Honey, drop her off somewhere and then get to London, England quick. Your mother saw Honey's picture and told the enforcers we knew her. Uncle Elmo is stalling but he'll have to lead them to you eventually. I told Mom you were visiting Great-Aunt Maud."

"Where Dad?"

"Don't tell me. Pick a spot that will leave you enough power to get to London. Quickly!"

Frederica stared down at the communicator blankly for several seconds. Considering she'd had to show Frederica where they were on a map the last time she visited, Honey was certain the girl had no clue what place was midway between there and London.

"Rome, take me to Rome," Honey said, pulling up a map of Europe in her mind.

"I've never been to Rome."

"But you've seen pictures of the buildings, right? The Pantheon?"

Frederica shook her head.

"The Colosseum?"

Another shake.

"The Leaning Tower of Pisa, which isn't in Rome, but is in Italy."

Frederica scrunched her nose. "Leaning tower." She nodded sharply. "Okay, I've got it. Grab your stuff."

Honey grabbed Frederica's crown. All her stuff was safety anchored in the Nether. "I need to say goodbye."

"Quickly in Dad speak means 5 minutes ago."

Honey had never seen Frederica look so serious. She looked around for a pen and paper to leave a note, but there was nothing. She'd have to ask Brayton to tell Dr. Ziga to relay a thank you to his sister later. "Okay, I'm ready."

"Go."

Honey stepped through the portal and was nearly blinded by the afternoon sun shining off the light-colored stone of the tower in front of her. Before her eyes could adjust, she was knocked to her knees.

Frederica rolled off her and immediately turned to face the wall they'd popped out of. "Sorry Honey. Good Luck. I've got to keep going."

"Thanks Frederica."

Frederica vanished into the wall. Honey picked herself up off the ground, trying to act like it was perfectly normal for her to have been kneeling there in the first place. The ancient-looking wall behind her partially surrounded a large courtyard that held both the leaning tower and what appeared to be a large church. Despite all the people milling around the tower, no one was pointing or whispering in her direction. How had they not noticed Frederica in a fluffy pink tulle dress appear and then disappear into the wall?

Honey bent down and picked up the object glinting at her from the ground. Frederica had forgotten her crown.

She let out a long sigh and sent the crown to the nether. She was on the run, again. Okay, assess the situation. She was alone in Italy and decently clean since she'd had a shower after they'd finished the last rice field. The sun was shining, it was warmer but not as wet as Nepal, and she had all her supplies. No one knew she was a witch or wolf at this moment and hopefully, there were no cameras monitoring the wall she was against. She reached behind her and pulled her backpack from the nether like she'd practiced in the mirror. From the front it would look like she'd just pulled it off her back. From the side, not so much.

She pinned on the charm her grandmother had given her to hide her wolf side from the witches, then slipped on the wristband with the charm she'd made to hide the lying scent of the necklace from the wolves. Next, she donned a black, nondescript baseball cap and a pair of sunglasses. That should work for now. Her next step was to find a place to sleep. Dad had mentioned young people could travel across Europe cheaply by staying in hostels or by camping, sometimes for free. Considering where she was, there had to be a hostel somewhere. She only had to figure out where it was. That meant she needed a library or maybe a hotel. They usually had computers.

She eyed the line leading into the tower. If she got in line with the tourists, she could climb the tower and get a bird's eye view of everything, or she could follow that plane passing behind the tower that looked like it was going to land. An airport surely meant hotels. She slung her backpack over her shoulder and headed for the road.

She was almost to the pavement when a sudden thought stopped her in her tracks. Frederica could portal to her no matter where she was. After what had happened to Brayton, she'd forgotten to add a spell against portals to her protective hairband. If the enforcers got to Frederica, they might find a way to force her to find Honey. She needed to make another shielding spell, but how did you make one against portalling? There had to be a way, otherwise bad witches would portal into banks and other places they shouldn't all the time.

Forcing her feet to move again, Honey thought of everything she'd read and learned in the past couple of months on shielding and portalling. To portal, you needed a target and something solid to anchor to and enough magic to bend space to bring the ends together. If she could somehow freeze the process or prevent the fold, yeah, she had no idea how to do that.

Her anti-scrying spell used broken pieces of mirror to confuse anyone trying to look for her. Maybe she could spread some of her molecules so a portal wouldn't know where to latch on. Right. There was no way she could disperse enough to distract from her body, not without harming herself.

Would a simple layered shield work? No, the portal didn't appear on her, it appeared near her, so she couldn't just slough off the surface. If she could just…oh. She could freeze the molecules as a portal started to open! If the molecules couldn't move, the door couldn't form. All she had to do was adjust a shield charm to detect portal magic instead of harmful magic and combine it with a freeze charm. She paused near a big statue in the middle of an open square to retrieve a red hairband from her backpack. As normally as she could, she lifted the band to her lips and blew her spell into the elastic, then slid it on her wrist. Too bad she didn't have a way to test it.

3

BRAYTON – JULY 21 – INDIANA

What was that annoying noise? Oh, his phone. Brayton picked it up and squinted at the number. A spammer at this time of night? What was wrong with people? He hung up and rolled over. A few seconds later the noise started again. Releasing a few choice words under his breath, he groped for his phone and flipped it over so that it hung up. The silence lasted for all of a breath before it started again. Maybe it wasn't spam. He glanced at the screen again. It was a local number, so not Honey, but if it would shut them up... He swiped up, then put the phone to his ear.

"What?"

"Hello to you too, Brayton."

"Who is this and why are you calling at such an ungodly hour?"

"What are you, an old man? It's only 2 am and there's a full moon. It's Damien."

"What do you want?"

"Grumpy much? I need to talk to Honey."

Like he would let Damien anywhere near her, not after he and his twin brother, Deacon, had competed to win her affections because of a stupid contest set forth by their dad even though she was nearly ten years younger than them.

"Honey? Why?"

Was she safe? She'd missed their time. He'd checked to see if she'd written as often as he could, but he could only go to the bathroom so many times before Mom got suspicious.

"Is she there?"

"Of course not. That would be stupid."

"Do you know how I can contact her?"

"What do you need?"

"Remember that curse my brother put on me?"

How could he not? Brayton had been shocked to discover alpha powers could be taken away. Even more shocking was that Damien's own brother had done it to him.

"Curse? I thought it was a spell."

"Either way, my powers are still bound."

"I thought you were going to go to the Witch Council."

"They said since the spell was put on me at the request of a wolf it was not a Council matter and that I should speak with my alpha."

"Ouch."

Unlike any other alpha in the world, Damien's dad had been impressed by Deacon's means of gaining more alpha power even though he took it from his own twin brother.

"What about your mother?" Brayton suggested, "Maybe she could speak to the witch who put the spell on you and…"

"Ma couldn't convince a tree to give her a nut even if the nut fell on her head," Damien interrupted.

Wow, hurtful, but he wasn't surprised. Damien's mother was quiet and meek and tended to blend into the background during social functions.

"I don't see what Honey has to do with it."

"Stop playing dumb, Brayton. I saw the news. She's a curse breaker. I want her to break the curse."

"She can't exactly roam around in public right now. Did you know the Enforcers searched our property?"

"Brayton, I'll do anything, go anywhere."

"Damien, no offense, but I don't trust you. There's a reward for her capture. Also, I'm pretty sure my phone is bugged."

Was it his imagination or had he heard a faint beep?

"You're probably right about the bug thing, but not about me. I mean Honey no harm. I don't care what she is as long as she can break the curse, and if she can break the one on me, that's proof enough that the hybrid curse doesn't apply."

"I can't help you, Damien. I don't know where she is. The Enforcers might have her by now. I'm going back to sleep."

"Hey, I heard about what happened," Damien said before Brayton could find the button to hang up, "You good?"

Damien truly sounded concerned. Brayton reluctantly put the phone back to his ear.

"I'm fine. You don't think what happened to me was due to her curse?" he asked curiously.

"Do you?"

"No."

"That's good enough for me. You want to catch up sometime?"

"Really?"

If anyone *was* listening they'd know right away Damien just wanted to speak in person.

"I know, I know, I'm an ass. I just thought…never mind."

"Sure. I need to get used to the eye patch. Wanna go to the track tomorrow?"

"Eye patch?"

"Yeah. Cici calls me cyclops."

"You lost an eye?"

"Hard to grow it back when it's completely burned away," Brayton said as nonchalantly as he could.

"I didn't realize it was that bad."

"Yeah. I probably would have died if Honey hadn't shown up and knocked the witch out. It was the same guy who murdered her parents, you know. She had nightmares when we first found her. She saw them burning, but it was too late to save them. I'm worried that she'll have nightmares again and she's all alone." He was going to start crying himself if he wasn't careful.

"O…kay."

"TMI? Sorry. Not quite awake. We'll be there at 9 am. See you or not. Night."

He hung up the phone and tossed it on the bed and waited. After several minutes and his mother still hadn't charged into the room demanding he not go to the track, he decided his mother must have gotten tired of monitoring his calls and fallen asleep. He rolled out of bed and headed for the bathroom. The hallway was clear. The bathroom was clear too. He even checked the shower before locking the door and squatting to retrieve the slate from where he'd relocated it to the cabinet under the sink.

31

"Brayton, are you in there?"

He quickly retracted his hand and stood to grab his toothbrush. "Yeah Mom, what's up?"

"We need to talk."

Shoot, he'd left the cabinet open. That would make her suspicious. He closed it as quietly as he could, then unlocked the bathroom door. "About what?"

"You're just now brushing your teeth? I thought you went to bed."

"I forgot to brush them. What do you need."

She shook something at him. "I found this in the pocket of your pants."

"The ones I wore today?"

"Yes. It's a hairband with a heart on it. Is this Honey's?"

"No, it's mine."

"Don't lie to me, Brayton Mooney."

"I'm not. Honey gave it to me."

"Is there something going on between you?"

"No Mom. That's a shield charm. Honey gave one just like it to Alpha Silver and his guards. The guard that got hit with the death spell would have died if he hadn't been wearing it. If I'd been wearing mine," he pointed to his eye, "this wouldn't have happened."

"Did she make it?"

"She didn't say. She just handed them out to us before we broke the curse. She was afraid the witches were after her and she didn't want any of us to get hurt."

"Why weren't you wearing yours?"

"This," he pointed to his eye again, "happened later after I went for a run. I didn't wear it because I was stupid.

The guard was smart. I should have worn it. I knew there might be witches around."

"How does it work?"

"It's automatic. If it detects a witch trying to harm me, it turns on. It won't last forever. I smelled the guard's give out when the curse hit him, but it was enough to save his life."

His mom let out a loud sigh and handed the hairband to him. "I guess you can keep it if you're not using it to communicate with her."

"I'm not. I just want to be prepared. Mom, I know you're worried about the curse, but I don't think Honey is what you should focus on. The curse can be broken. If the curse is broken, then it won't matter what Honey is. Do you really want her to die? I thought you liked her."

"You are my son, Brayton. You come first."

"Then help me save her Mom. I don't want her to die."

"You did at one point."

"No. I never wanted her to die. I just wanted her to show some respect like everyone else. I demanded it and she refused." He still couldn't believe what an immature brat he'd been back then. "You, on the other hand, earned her respect."

"Great, I earned the respect of a monster."

He was tired of fighting with her. "Name calling is beneath you. Good night, Mom." He wiggled his toothbrush. "I'm going to finish getting ready for bed."

He brushed his teeth, then locked the door and used the restroom before he finally reached under the cabinet for the slate. His heart leapt to see lines other than the ones he'd written looping across the gray surface.

Had to move. Schedule unknown. I'll keep checking.

He desperately wanted to ask what had happened, but the less he knew the less he could be forced to say. Instead he wrote,

Damien heard about your skill on TV. Wants your assist. Told him nothing. Stay safe little wasp. ((()))

4

HONEY – AUGUST 5 – ITALY

Honey put the mop away and hung her apron on one of the large wooden pegs in the broom closet.

"Where are you off to today, Belle Ragazza?" the woman behind the front desk asked.

Although she didn't feel particularly beautiful today, Honey smiled at her host and pulled a travel brochure from her pocket.

"The *Passeggiata Anita Garibaldi*," she read.

"Oh-a, yes, that is a very bellissimo path. You will be careful."

"Always, Signora Falsone."

She'd only known the kind woman for two weeks, but she would miss Signora Falsone when she left. Did she really need to move on after only two weeks though? She'd picked that length of time because it seemed like a good compromise between staying hidden yet not so long that she'd start to put down roots and endanger others or risk someone identifying and reporting her. In the last two weeks though, other than a few wolves who'd stayed at the hostel for one night and some magic she smelled in the bathroom, she hadn't run across any other wolves or witches. The hostel was in a good location and for only a few hours of work, she was able to pay for her room and board and still have plenty of time to explore. Genoa was not only beautiful, it was old, really old – like fifth century BC old. She hadn't found one yet, but there had to be a witch library or a magical collection somewhere with information on the hybrid curse.

Was her effort worth it though? Even if she did find the name of the fifth family, would anyone care? According to Brayton and Nathan, not a single witching family had expressed an interest in destroying their part of the curse since her grandmother had read off the names to the council. Now she could see how foolish it had been to think any of them would. She was one person and a mutt at that. It was easier to get rid of her than to fix a problem most of them didn't even consider a problem. The increasingly frequent feeling of hopelessness swamped her, weighing her down, making her feel like she was wearing weights around her ankles while she climbed the stairs.

Letting her wolf out would make her feel better. The thought of locking herself into one of the aged, well-used bathrooms in the hostel for a few minutes made her cringe though. It would be the smart, safe thing to do, but outside was so much nicer. She stopped her up-stair slog to peer out a window. Below, a shaggy-looking mutt was trying to charm a young woman into sharing the gelato in her hand. She could be that mutt. Her wolf was small enough she would blend right in with all the strays roaming everywhere and if she wore her charms, there was no reason any witches or wolves should suspect she wasn't simply a wolf-like dog.

She pulled out the map she'd printed at the library to study the trail one last time. The free beach she planned to run to was on the smaller side, but not so small that everyone would be paying attention to each other. What if...would it be safe to transform there? She doubted any beaches commonly used by witches or wolves would be offered freely to humans. Wouldn't hurt to take a look.

In the bathroom, she changed into a bathing suit and running shorts, covered those with a long flowing skirt and a loose blouse, then hid her hair with a head scarf and her eyes with dark sunglasses. Luca would tease her about looking like an old lady if he could see her, but the scarf did an excellent job of hiding her hair and scarves weren't uncommon here. Besides, she only planned to wear it until she reached the trail.

Before she put her bag back into the nether, she pulled out her two remaining magic slates. She still felt bad about destroying Frederica's and missed her random and usually silly comments but she was pretty sure someone had found it. Even Frederica would have never written, "*Hi Honey, where are you?*" especially since they'd all agreed not to use their real names.

Liam's slate was blank which meant he'd gotten her last message but had nothing new to share. Brayton's, on the other hand, was full.

Hey stinger. Court today. Gaian guilty of two counts of attempted murder. Tried to claim self-defense. Wolves shot that down. Twenty years and his powers bound, not that there was a choice in that. I testified how you saved me. Your Gma slipped me her number. She says hi and she loves you. Stay safe. ((()))

She'd never felt so lonely before, not even in Canada or right after her parents' deaths. If it wasn't such a stupid idea, she'd use one of the portals Alpha Silver had given her before she'd gone to Nepal so she could get a real hug. Instead, she drew a happy face and a talking bubble with '*Yay!*' inside, then a really big hug ((((((()))))).

Running with a bathing suit turned out to be very convenient. All she had to do was slip off her shorts, discretely send them with her shoes and socks to the nether, and walk into the water. Maneuvering in the crowded water was another story. After making it past little kids with buckets and shovels, she dodged three ball-wielding teens and an extremely large man who was paying absolutely no attention to where he was floating. It wasn't until the water was up to her neck that she could see more water than skin. The good news was, all her fellow swimmers smelled human.

With all the people around to distract the lifeguard, her plan to transform for a few minutes might just work. She only had to find a place to disappear for a moment – perhaps behind the buoys. She glanced back. No one was paying any attention. A buoy was just a bit further. It had been years though since that summer her mom had rented the house with a pool and taught her to swim. Plus, that water hadn't had waves.

She could do this. There were little kids out there. If they could be brave, so could she.

She floated forward, then sank until her toes touched the sand again. The water was up to her mouth. Another bounce and it was up to her nose. The buoy was still tens of yards away. How deep was it out there? Another bounce and she couldn't see above the water without floating. This was a bad idea.

Something hit the back of her head. She turned to see what it was and got a face-full of yellow vinyl that continued to plow over her until she was completely underwater. She flailed her arms and just managed not to bump the tropical fabric-covered bony rear in the middle of the inner tube. Rude. Well, since she was here...she did her best to push herself a few feet below the surface, which turned out to be remarkably difficult – due to the salt perhaps? - then transformed under water.

She'd forgotten how much easier it was to swim as a wolf. Sure, she couldn't go as fast, but staying above the water was simpler. She paddled close to the kid in the yellow raft so the lifeguard, who was currently distracted by a talkative girl in a very skimpy suit, would think she belonged to someone if he ever looked up. After a few minutes, three other kids joined the first. One of them threw a floating stick-toy at her. Since no adults yelled to tell him he shouldn't play with a strange dog, she retrieved it. The other kids joined in, racing her to the stick when the kid threw it again. They kept beating her, but it was fun, probably the most fun she'd ever had in the water. For a moment, the lonely ache in the center of her chest faded.

It didn't last. The sun disappeared behind the buildings and the kids' parents started calling to them. One-by-one, the children left without looking back, leaving her alone again. She made sure they all left the water safely, then turned and paddled toward a large rock jutting into the side of the swimming area which looked like a promising place to transform and climb out. She was about ten feet away when screaming from the sandy shore snagged her attention.

The lifeguard took note at the same time Honey changed direction. Most of the words the woman spewed toward the lifeguard were lost on Honey, but one word was clear – bambina – baby. The people on the beach who were near the scene started looking around. Had the woman lost her baby? Honey really needed to be on her way, but she couldn't just leave if there was a baby missing. She swam toward the shore, keeping her head underwater as much as she could in case the child was under the waves. She made it all the way to the shore without spotting anything except two shoes, not matching, and a pair of goggles. The sun was low enough now that the beach was covered in shadow. People were still looking, but not as many as before. She climbed out and shook herself, then jogged over to the woman who was still frantically calling out the child's name between sobs.

The woman didn't even notice Honey until she was close enough to touch her with her nose. The woman smelled like sunblock and sand and sweat and magic. Shoot. With her grandmother's charm on the hairband around her wrist, the witch shouldn't be able to tell what she was, but it wasn't smart to put herself in a position where she could be discovered. She'd already done that twice and now the whole world was looking for her.

The woman jumped when she noticed Honey and slapped at her nose. "Scappa!"

Honey sat down and whined.

"Oh, sei un…"

Honey barked.

"Un cane da salvataggio."

Honey had no idea what that meant, but the woman looked hopeful, so she barked again.

"Venire!" the woman said, waving her hand to show that Honey should follow her, and ran toward a towel and a bag on the beach. She pulled out a cute little dress and held it in front of Honey's nose while spitting out a string of words.

Honey memorized the scent and started sniffing around the towel. The ground around was coated with the little girl's baby powder smell. She worked in wider and wider circles until she found a trail that went off without the mother's scent. The girl's scent went away from the water and straight up the wide trail that led away from the beach and to a small boat parked with several others. Honey put her paws up on the edge and looked in. She had no idea how the little girl had crawled into the boat, but she was there, sleeping on the bottom. The mom pushed past Honey with a sob. Honey backed away. One of the other women who had followed the mother started shouting toward the beach, Honey assumed to tell people the child had been found. Nobody was paying attention to her. Time to go.

Out of nowhere, something dropped down over her head and tightened around her neck. Now what? Two men in blue coverall uniforms stood behind her. Wolves. She should have been paying more attention. She tilted her head at them as if to ask what they were doing on the off chance that if she came across as an intelligent dog, they'd think she belonged somewhere. Unfortunately, their response was in Italian. They didn't sound mean at least. Maybe she could convince them someone was waiting for her. She pointed her nose toward the beach and whined. The man holding the catch pole shook his head and said more words. Okay, option B. She barked. The witch, who had been walking back to the beach with her baby in her arms, looked back and appeared for a moment like she was going to protest. The man with the catch pole spoke sharply to her. The woman looked apologetically at Honey, released a string of words, then walked away.

Plan C it was.

Honey pretended she was compliant while the men pulled her toward a small truck with a covered back big enough to hold a small bear. She even pranced a little and wagged her tail like she had no reason to be upset or afraid. In response, her captor tightened the noose around her neck. Not nice. She waited until the second guy had reached up to unlock the back of the truck before she froze them and made the rope around her neck vanish. She stepped forward just enough for the rope to not reconnect with the pole, then willed it back out of the nether. As soon as the now disconnected loop of rope fell from her neck, she took off, simultaneously unfreezing the wolves so they wouldn't suspect any magic. She was past the first building before they realized their catch pole was broken and started shouting at her.

Did they realize she was a wolf or had they simply been doing their jobs as dog-catchers? If this was their territory, there were probably other wolves waiting down the path who might step in and help recapture her. They would be expecting a dog to run by, not a human. She stopped in a spectator-free area by a building and transformed. Barefoot, in her bathing suit, and covered by her airshield, she calmly walked toward the beach while the dogcatchers searched around her. After stepping under one of the free showers along the beach just long enough to rinse off the worst of the salt from her skin, she made sure she was downwind from the wolves she could still smell and pulled her running shoes and shorts from the nether.

A few yards back up the path, she noted three wolves: one jogging and two walking and gesturing at each other. She stepped to the side and tried not to look like who they were searching for. Spotting a woman with a stroller only a few feet ahead of her, she sped up. The wolves were looking for someone alone, if she struck up a conversation with the woman, they'd be less likely to suspect her, assuming they had somehow known she was a wolf.

The woman was hissing in a strange language, not Italian, under her breath. Honey hesitated, not wanting to interrupt her phone conversation. The wind shifted and she realized it was the same witch whose child she had just found. Phooey. There was no reason the woman should recognize her now, but better not to chance it. She allowed herself to get caught behind a slowly walking couple while someone passed from the other direction. The wolves had no reason to suspect her. With her air shield up they wouldn't even be able to smell the salt on her skin.

The baby started to cry.

The woman reached forward. Honey couldn't see what she did, but it sounded like skin hitting skin. The child's wailing abruptly ceased. Had the woman slapped that cute little girl?

Honey zipped around the slow couple and jogged up to the woman. "Pardon me, I've gotten a bit lost. Can you tell me how to get to the museum?"

"Which one?" the woman said kindly. She had a mild accent, but Honey couldn't place it.

43

"Umm, art."

"They will all be closed now."

"I know. If I can find the museum, I can get back to my hostel."

"Don't you have a phone?"

"Not with a working battery," Honey fibbed.

"How *ghayr maswuwl* of you."

"What does that mean?"

"Brave. How brave of you to travel alone without a working phone."

"Oh. Thanks. I find it's generally more fun when I travel to talk with the locals than look at my phone."

"Are you traveling alone?"

Honey faked a laugh. She knew better than to answer that with a yes. "Just jogging alone. How old is your baby?"

The streetlamps lining the path were bright enough that Honey could tell one side of the baby's face looked redder than the other. The woman *had* slapped her. What was surprising was that the baby had quieted instead of crying more. She looked like she wanted to. In fact, the wide, tear-filled eyes watching Honey looked scared.

"How old does she look?"

"I am not a good judge of age. Two?"

"Close enough. I'm in need of an emergency babysitter tonight. Do you have a couple of hours free?"

Was this woman crazy?

"You don't know me."

"No, but I'm an excellent judge of character. The fact that you pointed out that you are a stranger just proves it. Look, my husband is out of town and I need to go to the store but I know if I take her with me it will be a disaster.

She's already fussy and she'll just have a meltdown. I'll give you thirty euros to watch her for two hours."

The mom was blatantly lying to her, but about what: the husband, the shopping, the baby, or the pay? Was it her imagination or had the baby shook its head at her?

"I'm sorry. I don't have two hours. I have to get back to the hostel before they close the doors."

"One hour then. Just one. Please. I just need to get some diapers."

Another lie. "Um.."

"And get out of the house. I love my daughter, but I need some adult time."

Still lying. Did she not love her daughter?

"Okay, as long as it's not far. I really need to get back."

"I have a computer. You can look up where you need to go."

Another lie. Did the woman not have a computer? Why would she lie about that? The little girl now looked extremely sad. Honey had a sudden, very strong suspicion that the little girl had escaped on purpose. She looked too young to know how to run away, but what if she had and Honey had foiled her plan?

"That's kind of you," Honey thought to say while discretely feeling her wrist to make sure her anti-evil magic spell charm was still there.

"My house is just up this path."

Something was off. It was undoubtedly foolish to follow her, but the woman couldn't know who or what she was and she'd messed up the little girl's escape plan, if that's what it had been. Honey discreetly tested the air while the woman led her down a road lined with palm-tree

45

shaded sidewalks and neatly trimmed bushes so thick you couldn't see the houses behind them. She didn't smell anything magical but that just meant the woman wasn't using magic right now. After a couple of blocks, the woman stopped in front of one of the iron gates in the hedge. "Here we are."

There were no spells around the gate that Honey could see or smell, nor around the property. It wasn't until the woman unlocked the door that she smelled it, dead mouse. The woman's power was necromancy.

5

HONEY – AUGUST 5 – ITALY

Having powers of necromancy did not make a witch bad. The ability to manipulate essential life forces meant they could share their energy to add strength to the spells of other witches. They could also animate things like paper birds to fly on their own much like conjurers. It was the witches who stole the life forces of other organisms to power their spells that gave necromancers a bad name, along with those who animated the dead, but they were usually the same people.

Is that what this witch was, an evil necromancer?

The woman parked the stroller by an umbrella stand and turned to Honey with a kind smile. "I didn't catch your name."

"Heidi."

"Very nice. I'm Marisa and this is Giselle." She lifted the baby out of the stroller by her armpits and offered her to Honey. "Here. Your hour starts now. She needs a diaper change. Her room is up the stairs to the left. I'll be back. If you have any problems, go next door."

"Okay."

It was possible the woman wasn't evil and that Honey had misinterpreted what she'd seen and heard. Still, she kept her ears opened while she carried the sopping wet baby upstairs. Marisa left with a slamming of the door before Honey was even halfway up the stairs.

The baby's entire bottom half was wet.

"I think you need more than a diaper change."

The baby's room was painted a creamy white with cute pastel animals behind a cheery yellow crib. The furniture, including the changing table and a large dresser, all matched. Honey set the baby on her feet near the changing table and opened the dresser. The kid had more clothes than she'd ever had in her entire life.

"Okay, what are you in the mood for, a dress, shorts, tights?" She peered around the dresser door to see what the baby was doing. The baby was gone.

Honey turned just in time to see the kid's sandy pink pants disappear through the bedroom door. She sprinted and managed to catch the baby at the top of the stairs.

"You're fast. Maybe we can run some laps after we get you cleaned up. You can't be comfortable in that. I'm still a bit wet myself and I'm not comfortable, but at least my suit will dry."

"Run!"

"You can talk!"

"Run!"

"Okay, after we get you changed."

She carried the little girl into her room and grabbed the first outfit she saw before laying her down on the floor to change her clothes. The girl wasn't wearing a diaper and her pants and underwear were full of sand.

"I think you need more than a change."

"Run!"

"Yes, we'll run, but you do not want sand in your underwear. Trust me. Do you like baths?"

The kid rolled to her feet before Honey could stop her, and ran into the hall, sans pants, much faster than Honey realized babies could move. Honey chased her into a bathroom that looked like it was stuck in the 1950's. Honey picked the toddler up and stood her in front of the faucet in the tub.

"I'll turn on the water and you tell me when it's warm enough."

The girl obediently put her hand under the faucet. Were two-year-olds usually this smart?

It took several minutes for the water to finally run hot. Thanks to the few days she'd spent with Zavier and his adopted son, she knew babies only needed a couple of inches of water. The child was very compliant, helpful even, nothing at all like Zavier's son who loved baths only as long as he was getting everyone else wet.

"Run?" the girl asked once Honey had her clothed.

"Sure. Shall we go downstairs? There's probably more room down there."

The baby jumped (jumped!) down from the changing table and landed on her feet. Honey caught a whiff of lemon when she lunged after her, and something less pleasant.

"You have telekinesis and necromancy?" Honey asked.

The baby stopped at the head of the stairs and looked at her with wide eyes. The kid probably had no idea what she was talking about. Witches usually only had one talent, although there were exceptions, like herself. There was another option though.

"Is there a spell on you?" Honey switched to her other sight. There was something surrounding the baby in the space between the molecules. It looked like she was standing in the belly of a short, fat snake.

The child put out her hand. "Run."

"You do have a spell on you," Honey said, taking the girl's hand. "What does it do?"

The baby tugged her down the stairs.

The head of the snake lunged but just as quickly bounced back. Honey caught the faint scent of her own magic. Her protection charm was working but what was the spell for? All she could smell was death and baby powder.

"Is the spell bad?" Honey asked when they reached the bottom step.

"Bad," the girl agreed and pointed toward the door. "Run."

"Would you like me to break it first?"

The girl stomped her little foot. "No! Run!"

"Okay, okay, but I'm not sure your mom would want us to go outside."

"Bad mom. Run. Now."

"Okay. I suppose it will be fine if we just run up and down the sidewalk. You need shoes."

The girl immediately ran to the entryway and started pulling on a small pair of sneakers. Honey knelt down to help her, but the child did it all by herself with the help of the velcro tabs. Before Honey could pull open the front door, it opened to Marisa standing on the stoop with a bottle of wine.

"Everything okay?" Marisa asked.

"Fine. Has it been an hour?"

"No. You still have half-an-hour to go. I just came to drop this off. Were you two going somewhere?"

Another lie and it wasn't about the time unless Honey's watch was lying too.

"I thought she'd like to play in the yard a little," Honey lied back. "You have a yard, right?"

"It's very small, unfortunately. Her room is bigger. Why don't you take her up there and play until I get back. I don't want her to get dirty again before bed."

"Oh, sure."

Marisa shook her finger at the silent baby. "And you behave."

Honey picked up the baby and propped her on her hip. "She's no trouble at all. Go finish your shopping."

Honey could feel Marisa's eyes on her back all the way up the stairs, but didn't hear any movement. She carried Giselle into her room and shut the door but left it cracked so she could hear Marisa leave.

"Okay, what shall we play?" she asked Giselle.

The little girl plopped down next to a neatly organized row of stuffed animals and began listlessly flicking the floppy ears of a big dog.

"Ear flicking. Perfect. That's one of my faves. I get the bunny."

A door shut downstairs.

Honey leaned forward and whispered, "Think she's gone?"

"No run," the girl said sadly.

"Don't give up yet." Honey crawled back to the door and slowly looked out. Marisa was still at the bottom of the stairs, but she had her back to them. She suddenly jerked her head to look back over her shoulder. Honey quickly retracted her head so it was behind the door frame. A few moments later, Honey heard the front door shut.

After checking to make sure the woman wasn't sneaking up the stairs, Honey closed and locked the bedroom door, then plopped down in front of the girl. "Okay, let's work on that spell. It has a mouth and it looks like it ate you but you aren't digesting. It keeps trying to eat me. Does that mean it wants to multiply so we're both in its belly?"

The girl cocked her head. "Bad. Eat."

"I'm right about the eating part? Hmm. You know what this reminds me of? Little Red Riding hood. Have you heard the story?"

The little girl gave a slow shake of her head.

"The little girl in that story was eaten by a wolf. A woodcutter came and used his ax to cut her out of the wolf's belly. Let's see what happens. Don't worry, I won't use a real ax."

First, she gave herself a strong shield. She did not want whatever it was to deplete her charm in the middle of her attempt. The snake spell swelled and wove like it was trying to find a way past her shield. That was good. She pictured the top layer of her shield folding and forming a long, sharp edge right down the middle and sent it towards the girl. It shouldn't harm the child, but just in case, Honey said, "Hold perfectly still, okay."

The girl nodded.

The skin of the snake bent when the sharp edge of the shield hit it but still looked whole. The head of the spell barred its fangs and tried to bite the shield. Every bite felt like a hammer strike against a real shield, but Honey was encouraged by the spell's retaliation. It meant she was on the right track. She visualized the edge of the fin becoming even sharper and pushed it forward a little farther. The edge of the fin disappeared into the surface of the spell and something black and inky started to drip out. It worked! She imagined her shield blade splitting open down the middle to surround the baby and reseal behind her. Then, she reached in and pulled the girl into her lap, retracting the shield at the same time so that it formed a dome around them. The spell went wild, flailing all over the room and emitting black stuff and the nastiest smell she'd ever smelled. If it had been real, black would have coated the room.

"Can you see it?" she whispered to the girl.

The girl shook her head, but she was clinging to Honey like she was scared.

It might have gone on for more than a minute, but eventually, the spell started to slow, then gave a couple more flops, and dissipated, along with all the black.

That's when Honey noticed the baby in her lap wasn't a baby anymore. She was growing, and fast. Honey retracted the shield and scooted back. The girl's shirt tightened around her neck. Honey quickly banished her clothes to the nether, then averted her eyes when the child began to develop into a woman.

"You can look. After all the babysitters I've had, I'm not modest," a voice finally said.

"Well, I am."

Honey grabbed a blanket off the bed and tossed it toward the voice before finally looking. The baby had grown into a beautiful young woman with wavy blond hair and gorgeous light brown eyes.

"That was some growth spurt," Honey commented.

The girl snorted. "About time. I've been stuck in that form forever."

"How old are you?"

"I don't know, what year is it?"

"2024."

"Fifty-four then."

"Wow. You look amazing."

The girl looked down at herself. "My mom spelled me when I was eighteen. Is that the age I look?"

"Yes. Marisa is your mom?"

"Yeah."

"But she doesn't look old enough to have a fifty-four-year-old daughter."

"Magic," Giselle said, looking toward the door, "We need to get out of here before she comes back. She'll suck out your life to make herself young, or worse, use it to redo the spell."

"You'll need some clothes."

"Ha. Yeah, I guess I can't get away with running around naked anymore. I'll swipe some stuff from my mom's closet. Keep a lookout?"

"Sure. Grab some money if you know where it is. It will make things easier."

"Good idea."

What felt like ten minutes later, Giselle reappeared in the door at the other end of the hall in a short denim skirt, a crop-top, and an over-sized leather jacket. "Sorry I took so long. It took a while to find anything decent."

Honey decided not to comment on the 80's look the girl was sporting. "You have shoes?"

"My feet are bigger than my mom's"

"Sandals? Flip flops?"

"I think I saw something that might work. Hold on."

Giselle disappeared back into her mother's room. Honey heard the door open downstairs and quickly slipped out of sight.

"I'm back!" Marisa called.

Shoot, she was coming up the stairs. Honey ran down the short hall and into the mom's room and pulled the door closed behind her. Giselle looked up at her in horror. "We can't get away."

"You have telekinesis. Just jump out the window."

"They're spelled."

Honey bounced across the bed to reach the small window and threw it open, then took a deep sniff. "It's not."

"You're sure?"

"Yes. Go."

"Giselle, where are you? You know hiding the girl won't do any good."

"I can't just leave you," Giselle said.

"I'll be right behind you."

"She has a freeze stone."

"I can disable them. Go."

"Giselle!"

The door crashed open. Honey froze the woman, then leaped out the window to a handy branch. "You have twenty seconds Giselle," she yelled back.

She should have said ten, she thought ruefully while Giselle crawled slowly out the window, exposing her underwear to the world. At least she'd found some.

Honey was waiting on the ground by the time Giselle floated down.

"Run," Honey urged.

"No, let's take a taxi. I have money. I can't run in this skirt or these shoes."

Why had she let the girl dress herself? On the other hand, how was she supposed to know that the previously stylish baby would revert to 30-plus year-old fashion trends. "Okay, let's walk fast then and get out of here before your mom thaws." She grabbed Giselle's hand and dragged her toward the front gate. Where's the nearest bus station?"

"A bus?"

"They're cheaper and you'll need to buy better clothes and shoes."

"What's wrong with my clothes?"

"I'll explain when we're on the bus."

They got lucky. A bus was just pulling up when they emerged from the side road onto the main street. Honey ran ahead to hold it while Giselle walked – walked! – the few hundred feet down the sidewalk. In her defense, her shoes did keep sliding off her feet. The driver didn't seem to mind waiting, especially after Giselle gushed a thank you to him in Italian that included several flutters with her long curly lashes.

Honey pulled Giselle next to her onto a seat on the opposite side of the bus from where they'd emerged from the street. Sure enough, Marisa was already on the corner, waving for the bus driver to stop. Honey froze the driver's legs. He didn't act like he noticed, so perhaps he wasn't planning to stop anyway.

After only a few stops, the bus reached the end of its route and turned around. Afraid Marisa would be waiting for the return bus, Honey dragged Giselle out of the bus and headed for what looked like a park. Once they were hidden from the road by a large tree, she pulled her backpack from the nether and retrieved one of the portals Alpha Silver had given her.

"Giselle, it's dangerous for you to be with me. I have a friend who can shelter you though. He's a wolf. Is that okay?"

"My mom will come after him. She's dangerous."

"She'll have to find you first. He lives in the United States."

Giselle's face brightened. "Really? I've always wanted to go to the States. That was one of the things Mom and I were arguing about before she turned me into a toddler."

"Why did she do that?"

"She said she was tired of my backtalk and that I was a better daughter when I was two. She sucked the life out of my boyfriend to do it."

"I'm sorry."

"Me too. Weird to think he'd be an old man by now. She took another life every year to keep me young, and herself too."

"What did she do with the bodies?"

"I don't know. I'd guess she made them look like suicides or accidental drowning.

"That's awful."

How had no one noticed a pattern?

"Yeah, you were going to be next."

"Glad she failed."

"Me too."

They looked at each other for a moment, then Giselle pulled Honey into a tight hug. "Thank you. Thank you. Thank you. I'm in your debt forever."

Honey hugged her back and blinked away the unexpected tears. It had been weeks since she'd had a hug or any meaningful human contact.

"I assume you don't want to hide forever," she sniffed when Giselle finally released her.

"I don't."

Honey made herself smile at Giselle's concerned look. Stupid tears.

"Ask for Zavier when you get there, show him this," she pressed one of her protective charms into Giselle's hand, "then tell him your story. He'll be able to contact someone to help you. You're going to be popping out of a portal in the middle of his pack, so they might be a little wary and scary at first."

"You aren't coming with me?"

She wanted to, but Brayton had warned her that the Enforcers were monitoring all the locations Honey had been known to visit. "I can't. Don't tell anyone anything about me, except Zavier and only if he asks and he's the only one around, okay. Not a word. Don't mention me at all."

"Why?"

"Because I don't want to die."

"Die?"

"It's a long story and you need to go. Ready?"

"I guess."

Honey stood in front of a tree with the portal shell in her hand and pictured an outside wall of the shed just in case someone was sleeping inside. It was too dark to see the portal, but she could smell it.

"Go. Just walk into the tree. Quickly."

"Into the tree?"

"You have 3 seconds."

"Okay. Bye."

"Bye."

Giselle stepped through. Honey threw the shell after her to close the portal.

And she was alone again.

6

BRAYTON - AUGUST 7 - INDIANA

Dear Wasp,

[Aug 6, 10pm] I know what tomorrow is. (((((((((()))))))))). Imagine that's me holding you as long as you need. Z called. Said he now has a witch in his pack. She made it sound like the spell broke by itself but I know better. U R amazing. With love - BB.

BB, thank you for the hug and the news. Both are very much appreciated. Can you tell Gma about Z's witch? Witch's mom is a murderer and witch shouldn't have to keep hiding. [Aug 7, 6am]

Brayton sighed to himself. Honey was hurting, understandably. Today, or maybe yesterday for her, was the one-year anniversary of her parents' deaths. He wished with all his heart he could meet up with her somewhere in person, but he didn't know where she was. Zavier's new witch had come from Italy, but that was two days ago. Honey could have moved on. He hoped she had.

"Brayton, Damien is here."

It sounded like his mom was standing in front of his bedroom door.

"Brayton, are you in there?"

Brayton quickly erased Honey's words and scribbled a '*will do*', then slipped the slate into its new hiding place behind the medicine cabinet. He washed his hands, then sauntered out of the bathroom just as his mother came out of his room, carrying his phone.

"Find anything mom?"

She didn't bother looking hurt the way she had the first few times he'd caught her searching his room. "You had a couple of phone calls and some emails. How long were you in the bathroom?"

He took the phone and jammed it in his pocket without looking. "Not long. I haven't touched my phone all morning. I'm sure it's nothing important."

"What about the call from Damien?"

"What about it?"

"Did you know he was coming over?"

"Yeah. He told me he would last time he was here."

"I don't like that boy. Why are you hanging out with him?"

"One, he's an excellent fighter and he's helping me get used to the eye patch. Two, he doesn't have his alpha powers anymore so he's not a threat to anyone here. Three, he thinks I'm the key to Honey and breaking his curse. As long as he's coming over, you'll know he hasn't had contact with her. You should welcome him, Mom."

"Do you have contact with her?"

"Do you think I'd stay here and be grilled every moment of the day if I knew where she was?"

"That's not what I asked."

His mom thought he was avoiding the question so she couldn't smell his lie. He wasn't at all. Contact, in his opinion, was not scribbling words on an ancient child's toy. "I wish with all my heart that I did," he said truthfully.

"Brayton!"

He turned his back on her.

"Brayton, I've talked it over with your father. We both feel that you should take this semester off."

He looked back over his shoulder. "You mean *you* feel. Mom, I know you're worried about Honey contacting me, but we both know that you and the Enforcers are spying on me. You know which dorm room I'm staying in. You can install cameras next to the Enforcers' and watch me to your heart's content." He turned away to continue down the hall. "Why don't you hire someone to follow me around while you're at it."

"Brayton, that's not the reason," she said in her soft voice. When he didn't stop, she yelled, "You have anger issues."

He didn't bother replying. Of course he was angry. He was angry at her for being so hard-headed. He jogged down the stairs and into the large living room where Damien was waiting with Rhys. To his surprise, Dad was there too. He didn't believe for an instant that Dad had agreed with Mom about college. They'd talked about the classes he was going to take just yesterday, but Mom, as she always did lately, chose not to hear.

"Did you forget I was coming?" Damien asked.

"Nah, just lost track of time."

"Brayton, come see me when you're done."

"Sure Dad."

"Any news from Honey?" Damien asked once they were outside.

He still hadn't figured out Damien's angle. After everything that had happened last year, Damien had to know Brayton would never trust him, but the man persisted in meeting with him and asking about her. "I'm sure the world would have heard about it if I had."

"You sound bitter."

"I feel like every move I make is being watched and now my mom wants to chain me at home."

"You could just tell them where Honey is."

"Is that what you would do if you were me?"

Damien opened the door to the big barn that served as a gym. "I can't say I understand why you're protecting her. As a future alpha, your first responsibility is to your pack."

"She's part of my pack."

"For now. I'm surprised your dad hasn't kicked her out."

"She can't help what she is."

"I know, but now that you know…"

"Kicking her out would make it look like we don't support her ideas. We do. We agree that a curse by witches should no longer dictate our laws. We want the witches to destroy the curse and the only way to do that is present a strong front and keep hammering at them until they do something."

"Meanwhile, everyone who's heard of her is cursed."

Brayton plopped down on a mat to stretch. "Honey is a curse breaker. She broke that curse as it pertains to her when she was born. However, believing they are cursed should encourage the witches to destroy the curse. But that will only work as long as Honey is alive."

Damien sat down beside him. "Supporting her is a political move against the witches?"

It was much more than that to Brayton, but Damien didn't need to know. "Yes."

"Do you have a way to contact her?"

"I wish. Do you know what today is?"

"August 7th?"

"Her parents were killed one year ago today. Don't you think it's sad that she has to face that all alone? I do."

"She shouldn't exist."

"But she does." Brayton popped to his feet. "Come on, I'm feeling the need to kick you."

Damien snorted. "Keep dreaming."

Two hours later, after a frustrating session with Damien and a long, calming shower, Brayton took the back stair to Dad's office so he wouldn't have to pass Mom's. His dad, for once, was alone in his office.

"You wanted to speak to me, Dad?"

"Yes. Close the door and have a seat."

Closing the door meant it was serious. Brayton did as instructed, then leaned forward in his chair. "What's wrong?"

His dad stood and walked around the desk to sit in the chair beside him. "Your mom wants you to skip this semester. What do you think of that?"

"It's a stupid idea. I'll get behind all my friends and there's no reason I should. I just lost an eye, not my brain."

"I agree." His dad leaned back in his chair and sighed at the ceiling.

"Is that what you wanted to tell me?"

"She also wants me to banish Honey from the pack."

"No! We can't drop our support now. We need the witches to know we're serious."

"I agree with that too." His dad sighed again, then turned his head toward Brayton with a sad smile. "While I don't agree with your mother, I understand where she's coming from. I hated watching your struggle this past year. I felt helpless at times, but you've come out stronger and more mature at your age than I ever was. I'm very proud of you. Your mother doesn't see that yet and insists on blaming herself. I'd like to propose a compromise."

"What?"

"Why don't you take all your classes on-line for a semester?"

"On-line?"

"Yeah. You could drive up to campus on the mornings you have WOLF."

"Dad, you know she just wants to keep me under her thumb so she can spy on me, right?"

"She's not spying on you Brayton."

"Then why does she keep searching my room?"

His dad opened his mouth, then his shoulders dropped. "I didn't know she was doing that. I'll talk to her. If I can get her to agree to stop, will you agree to the on-line classes?"

"It doesn't matter. There's nothing there to find. I just wish she wasn't so hateful towards Honey. Honey didn't do anything. She can't help what she is."

"She lied to us Brayton."

"No. She just didn't tell us everything, for very good reasons. What would you have done if she told you right off that her parents were a witch and a wolf? She'd be dead. You would have done the same in her situation. I would have."

"I know and that's why she's still part of our pack. Unfortunately, it's going to cost us. The Joint Council has just levied a one million dollar fine against us."

"For what?"

"Harboring a hybrid."

"But we aren't. We don't even know where she is."

"She's a part of our pack, therefore we are responsible for her."

"If you kick her out, will they drop the fine?"

"It's already been imposed, so I doubt it."

"Would they drop it if we turned her in?"

"That's what they're offering."

"Would you turn her in if you knew where she was?"

His dad shook his head with a wry grin. "Nope. I knew it was going to get dirty when I didn't eject her. They're scared of the curse. This is where we hold our ground until they realize we're serious about getting rid of the curse altogether. Alpha Silver and Alpha Shane are with us and will help us fight the fine and get the witches on the right track. I've had calls from several other alphas offering their support as well. It's going to get ugly." He cracked his knuckles. "Too bad it probably won't come to blows. That would be fun."

"I can take my classes on-line Dad, if you think it would help with Mom. It would also save money on room and board."

"That it would. Thanks Brayton."

"Sure."

"Speaking of money, your name is on Zavier's land now, right? You took Honey's completely off?"

"Yes."

"Good. I'm sure the council would love to grab up anything in her name."

His dad stood and pulled him into a hug. "I love you, son."

"I love you too."

66

Mom was standing in the hallway with her fist raised like she was about to knock on the door, but Brayton knew better. She'd been listening or trying to. Since they hadn't been yelling, she wouldn't have heard anything.

It would serve her right if dad didn't fill her in, but he would.

Brayton couldn't remember ever being so mad at his mom for so long. She was worried. He knew that, but it didn't make it easier to face her. He turned away from her to look back into the room. "I'm going for a run, Dad. See you at supper."

His mom sniffed at him. "Didn't you just take a shower?"

Brayton ignored her and walked away, pulling his phone out of his pocket to look at it for the first time all day. There was nothing interesting, no strange numbers from foreign countries. It did give him an idea though. He pulled up Honey's grandmother's number and texted, "*Hi. It's Brayton Mooney. I heard you were one of the most powerful healers in the country. I've been told that nothing can be done for my eye, but I'd really appreciate your assessment. Would it be possible to meet sometime? Call anytime. I'll keep my phone on me. Thank you.*"

7

HONEY – AUGUST 16 – ROME

Dear Wasp.

[Aug. 15, 10pm]. Saw your Gma. Message passed. She looked at my eye too. Said she had some ideas on how to treat it but had to look some things up. Got all my classes switched except WOLF. It won't be the same without you. Stay safe. (((()))).

[Aug. 16, 8 am]. You mean because I won't be there to beat you on the obstacle course, turtle?

She checked her other slate one more time before tucking them both away. Still nothing from the boys. They'd either lost it or they'd decided it was safer not to write until they went back to class. One of Luca's nephews had nearly torn it up when he'd found it under Luca's bed.

She sighed and looked out the bus window at the buildings passing by. Was she doing the right thing? Her stomach hurt with nerves. She'd never had her hair done in a salon before. It should be safe. No one at the salon she'd picked smelled of witches or wolves. The girl she'd made the appointment with seemed competent and cheery, but she'd be exposing herself completely. If anyone recognized her, she'd lose any advantage she was about to gain along with the hair that had only ever been cut by her mom. Her mom had always loved her hair. Honey wiped away a tear. Her hair would grow back and it had to be done if she was going to accomplish anything. The witches would identify her on the spot if she tried to enter what she suspected was a magical library looking exactly like her picture. She just hoped they didn't have a way to detect the charm that hid her wolf side.

She was one of the first customers of the day. The cheery girl's eye's brightened when Honey removed her scarf.

"I love your hair."

"You'll buy it then, like we discussed yesterday?"

"Oh yes. What did you have in mind?"

Honey pulled out the picture she'd printed at the hostel.

"Ooo, a pixie-cut. That is a big change."

"I want the purple too."

"Of course."

It wasn't a lot of color, just a touch on the bangs and some on the back, but from what she'd observed while watching the front of the possible library, colored hair was a trend among the young witches in Rome just like it had been in Indiana.

The girl took Honey's heavy braid in hand. "You're sure?"

Honey nodded.

The girl made a quick cut, and just like that, Honey's braid was gone.

An hour later, she stumbled out of the salon feeling light-headed with her half-shaved head and pile of purple curls on top. She barely recognized herself. It was perfect. Now all she needed was the make-up to make her look older. She put on her sunglasses and wandered the streets like a tourist until she found a museum with a bathroom and a mirror, then followed the instructions she'd jotted down from the computer at a human library.

She was shocked. It actually worked. She looked at least eighteen.

She stepped out of the cool stone building into the paved everything and bright sunshine and immediately started sweating. Instead of walking the two miles to her next destination, she found another bus and rode it to within a block of the suspected library. Handily, there was a small café a few stores down from the library on the other side of the road. She purchased a bottle of *acqua minerale naturale* and sat down at a shaded outdoor table to monitor the door.

As far as she could tell, people just walked in. She was hoping to blend in with a large group but after thirty minutes and a second bottle, she'd only seen people entering alone or in pairs. It was time to do this, and not just to find a bathroom. She put her empty bottle firmly on the table and stood.

Three laughing teenagers walked by. One brushed against her shoulder and knocked her into the table. She didn't even stop to apologize. What was wrong with people?

A hand gripped her arm, pulling her up. "Signorina, are you okay?"

Honey looked up into the warmest brown eyes she'd ever seen set in a very handsome face.

"Si. Grazie."

There was a faint scent of magic around him, almost like a wolf, but not.

"I am Emmerico Meo."

"It's nice to meet you Emmerico Meo. May I have my arm back."

"Oh yes!" He released her elbow and took a step back. "An American! Are you visiting our fair city for the first time?"

"I am."

"Oh! You must allow me to show you around."

He was up to something, she was pretty sure, but she didn't think it was to turn her in. With her sunglasses, colored contacts, and her charms in place, he shouldn't be able to tell the color of her eyes or if she was a witch or a wolf. Maybe he knew something useful.

"What is that place?" she asked, nodding toward the entrance.

He looked between her and the door. "You can see it?"

"Of course."

"But that means," his nose wiggled, "you're a witch."

"Yep."

"Then you know what I am?"

"No. What are you?"

His eyebrows raised, then settled into what she could only describe as a playboy smirk. "Wouldn't you like to know."

It was more of a statement then a question, but she answered, "Yes, actually."

He nodded toward the door, "That's a history museum," then leaned toward her and whispered, "and I am a big, bad wolf."

He did smell more like a wolf now, but it smelled fake, like artificial vanilla flavoring versus the real thing. Plus, there was still a hint of magic, perhaps due to that wolf-shaped pendant peeking out from under the collar of his shirt.

A tanned hand blocked her inspection of the pendant.

"An heirloom." He cleared his throat. "You don't seem scared."

"Should I be?"

He waited for two people to pass, then asked softly, "How familiar are you with wolves?"

She had to be careful here. Most witches hardly knew any wolves, if at all. "Familiar enough. I went to school with some."

"Really?" he said doubtfully.

She nodded, "Some of the schools are integrated in the US."

"Huh. Well," he pulled up his playboy smirk again, "I can guarantee US wolves are not like me."

"Undoubtedly."

"And I can also guarantee you an excellent tour. It's what wolves do, after all."

"Tour?"

"No." He looked down the street and waved his hand like he was slowly wiping a large window, "Explore."

She chuckled politely at his overly dramatic sales pitch. "I think I'll stick with the museum."

"It's rather boring," he said earnestly.

"That's okay. I just drank two bottles of water. I'm not picky."

He blinked at her, then snorted. "They probably do have nice bathrooms."

"Wonderful. See you around Emmerico Meo."

72

She could feel his eyes on her back while she stepped through the door, but quickly became distracted by all the scents and sights inside. An anti-human ward and a bored looking young woman manning an information desk separated her from the displays, but no guards or scanners or any of the things she'd imagined. After paying ten euros for entry, Honey made a beeline for the toilette. The bathrooms were not only the cleanest she'd found in Italy, they also had magical plumbing. When she flushed, instead of washing away, stuff just disappeared, and when she waved her hands under the strange-looking faucet, they suddenly felt cool and clean with no water or soap involved.

The museum itself was amazing. It had all the things she'd read about in the history books and more. There was a grimoire from a Babylonian witch (one of the oldest in existence), three magic carpets, and an entire cursed tomb. The curse smelled deadly and she wondered how many people had died to get it to the museum. There were multiple displays demonstrating concepts like the importance of keeping magic a secret from humans (people had died) and the dangers of mixing certain powers (things exploded). Her favorite was an immersive display showing the rise and fall of famous witches over the ages. The witches literally rose from the ground like they were rising from a pop-up card, then fell flat on their faces and melted out of existence after they'd told their story. Luca would have found it gruesomely awesome. Curiously, not all the stories matched what she'd read. Whoever had made it must have read different books, or perhaps older ones?

About half-way through the display, five witches rose along with the sounds of wailing and burning piles of… bodies. The smell of burnt flesh was weak, but it was there. Honey covered her mouth and nose, but she couldn't stop her tears. Horrible things had happened throughout history, but did the display have to be so sensually accurate?

The witch with straight black hair streaked with gray stood taller. Honey forced herself to pay attention.

"We must do something. We must find a spell to cure this plague." The gold letters above her head formed the name 'Addela Bright'.

"It's not a plague, it's a curse," a man with tightly curled, oddly greenish hair and a full, frizzy white and tan beard said. His letters spelled out 'Edward Evelstone'.

"Who cast it?" Marie Lambert, a voluptuous young woman with golden, wavy hair and dirt on her cheek, inquired.

"It matters not. What's important is that we stop it. I have foreseen only one way to do so," a man with a heavy dark cloak trimmed in silver and a nicely trimmed goatee spoke. He didn't have any letters above his head.

"What? What did you see," the fifth person, labeled 'Ingunde Wixx', asked. Her gray-streaked brown hair was pulled back in a painfully tight bun.

"We must stop the intermarriage of witches and wolves."

"What does that have to do with it?" Marie Lambert demanded.

"The sullying of our blood with theirs is the cause of all this. We must cleanse ourselves of the impurity. All offspring resulting from such pairings must be destroyed and we must never allow it to happen again or we will all be wiped from the face of the Earth."

"What evidence do you have to support this claim?" Ingunde Wixx asked. Honey wanted to cheer for her ancestor.

"The plague started in Messina, and we all know what vile things go on there."

"That doesn't mean it was caused by them," Marie Lambert insisted.

"The mixed spawn of those who have dared to go against nature were the first to die," no-name said.

Honey doubted that. Hybrids would have healed faster than normal witches, but no one mentioned it.

"What can we do?" Addela asked.

"We must create a curse so horrible that witches and wolves will not even consider joining together again and we must ensure it can never be broken," no-name said.

"What are you proposing — that we sacrifice ourselves?" the Evelstone ancestor asked.

"No, nothing so drastic. We will ask every family, both witch and wolf, to add a drop of blood so that we can make a cure. We will use the blood to craft the curse and divide it among us so that the curse will be dispersed across the entire globe."

"There's got to be another way," Marie insisted. *"What about the curse breakers?"*

"It will take them too long. I have foreseen many outcomes. This is the only one where people survive."

He was lying. He had to be. The black death was caused by a bacterial infection, not magic, unless he was talking about some other plague that she'd never heard of. Honey walked closer to his form and sniffed. It was faint, but she could smell the seer magic on him, along with his sweat and smoke from the fires, but no lie. He either believed he'd seen it, or it was too faint for her to detect.

"I don't like this," Ingunde said.

"*We must do something or we and the humans will all die,*" Addela said. "*My healers are worn out. We can't keep up.*"

"*Good, it is decided,*" no-name declared. He whipped a scrap of paper out of his pocket. "*I've already written it down. All we need to do now is collect the blood, combine our powers, and imbue the curse on the appropriate vessels.*"

They all flipped face-down and another historical witch appeared.

Honey watched while witches went to the new world, were exposed in Salem, and fought the wolves in a remote part of Canada, but her mind kept going back to the scene of the curse. Who was that no-name person? Would breaking the hybrid curse truly cause everyone to be wiped from the face of the Earth? Was the plague really another curse? Did she need to break two curses? He'd also mentioned a town. Honey pulled her bag from the nether and retrieved her small notebook, then watched the display again and took notes.

Thirty minutes later, with her brain trying to conjure up answers to her many questions or places to get some, she stepped out of the room and failed in one of her dad's first lessens, pay attention to your surroundings.

"What did you think?"

Honey jumped and turned defensively toward the voice. An old woman stepped out of the shadows behind the door. She didn't look scary, but sometimes the oldest witches were the most dangerous.

"I have questions."

"I noticed," the woman said with a posh accent. She waved for Honey to follow and turned. "Come. We will have tea. It is not Babingtons, but it will quench your thirst."

Honey cautiously lowered the hand she'd put up to defend herself. "Babingtons?"

The old lady cackled but didn't stop her trek into the dark recesses of the hallway.

Was it safe? The woman didn't seem dangerous. Honey was certain she could take her in a non-magical fight. She touched the shield charm on her wrist to make sure it was there, then followed. The woman led her through a door with a 'staff only' sign written in multiple languages to a small room that looked like it belonged in the main museum as a display of a 19th century sitting room.

The woman pointed at a padded wooden chair with armrests on one side of a medium-sized round table. "Sit."

Honey obeyed. The woman tottered over to a side table and picked up a tray loaded with everything a person could want for tea including little triangular sandwiches without crusts, then turned toward the round table. Honey thought for sure she was going to drop it.

"May I help?"

"Stay. This is my exercise for the day."

The old lady did somehow manage to carry it across the small room and even sit it down with minimal rattling. She then proceeded to serve Honey just like Honey had seen in a couple of movies.

"This is nice," Honey said, pretending to take a sip out of the delicate cup the woman had placed in front of her. "Thank you for inviting me."

The woman cackled again, then took a sip out of her own cup. "Well, it's not often someone stays to watch my history all the way through twice in a row."

"Your history?"

"History the way I see it," the woman explained. "I'm a seer, but only of the past. That display is a collection of the most significant scenes I've seen over my lifetime. My dear husband, bless his soul, was able to craft a way for me to show them to other people. We started this museum together."

"It's a wonderful museum."

The old woman chuckled. "I'm glad you like it. Many do not like my version of history."

"May I ask you a few things?"

"That's why you're here."

"Why did some of the witches not have names?"

"Good question," the woman said, taking a pastry, "I don't see the names in my visions. Those were added later, after I did some research. If the name is missing, it's because I couldn't find it. Either I haven't looked in the right place or it was erased from history."

"Erased?"

"Yes. Witches often worked for kings and other rich folk. If they did something to displease their masters, the master might hire someone else to curse the witch so that their name was erased to history. Their own mothers would be unable to remember their names."

"Ouch."

"Indeed."

Honey took another fake sip. Was it safe to ask about the curse scene? Would the woman guess who she was? She might never get another chance to discover what really happened. "You said those were your most significant visions. Do you know what happened to the people who cursed everyone after the Black Plague?"

"I noticed you seemed particularly interested in that scene."

"You were watching?"

The woman gave a dainty shrug. "There's not much else for a woman of my years to do around here. In answer to your other question, they died."

"Because of the curse?"

"Maybe. I didn't see it. Everybody dies."

"Then you didn't see where they hid their parts of the curse?"

"I saw one of them hide the curse, but before I show you, tell what your interest is."

Honey couldn't think of a good excuse other than the truth. "I want to destroy them."

"Even though it might cause another plague?"

"I'm not sure it will. According to Mr. No-Name, the plague itself was caused by a curse, but he was very dismissive of trying to break it. I also got the feeling that he had a vendetta against mixed families. I need to do some research to be sure, but I don't think the curse was the reason the plague was finally defeated."

"And if it was?"

"Then I will revisit my goals."

The old woman chuckled. "For a youngster, you certainly have lofty ones. Why do you wish to destroy the curse?"

"Because all it has done is promote hatred and enough people have died. It's time to end it."

"Ah, to be young and know everything again. I will show you what I saw but I'm afraid it won't be very useful."

The old woman hoisted herself out of her chair and pulled a box the size of a tissue box off one of the shelves along the wall. She also retrieved what looked like a thick playing card. After setting the box in front of Honey, she inserted the playing card into a slot carved in the bottom front of the box. Bright lights glowed around the edges of the contraption and suddenly Honey was watching a miniature hologram.

Mr. No-Name stood in the midst of a circle of tall stones holding a square stone box about the size of a sauce pan with a stone lid. He lowered it carefully into a hole dug in the center of the stones, then started reciting something in a language Honey didn't recognize. From a silver tray on the ground next to the hole, he picked up a knife, sliced it across his palm, then continued reciting while his blood dripped into the hole.

Ten drops later, he turned and demanded in English, "Bury it."

A small boy, older than six but younger than nine, emerged from the shadows. His clothes were torn and dirty and his hair was standing up all over his head. Trails of tears had carved their way through the dirt smeared across his cheeks, although he wasn't crying at the moment. Keeping his head down, the boy obediently began to throw dirt on the box. He did a good job, even tamping the dirt down after he was through. Mr. No-Name lifted the knife and stabbed the boy in the back mid-tamp. Honey whimpered with the boy when he fell over the mound. Mr. No-Name utilized his knife several more times while muttering under his breath until the boy's body finally relaxed into death. The vision dissolved. Honey wiped her cheeks.

"Do you know what he was saying?" she asked the old woman who had gripped her shoulder while she was watching.

The woman didn't answer. Honey looked behind her to find the woman's head thrown back and her eyes shockingly white.

Honey removed the woman's hand from her shoulder and turned around in case she needed to catch her. "Are you okay? Should I get someone?"

The old woman took a sudden, deep breath and blinked. Her eyes were back to normal when Honey next saw them, except she looked troubled. The woman turned her back on Honey and started searching her shelves.

"You asked what he was saying. I don't know, but I wrote it down. The spelling is probably completely wrong." She grabbed a novel-sized notebook and thrust it at Honey. "You'll find it in there."

"What page?"

The woman shook her head. "Keep it. I started having visions regarding the curse the same year you were born. I saw your birth. I watched you grow up. I didn't have any visions last year, but now I understand why." A tear trickled down her cheek. "Sometimes I wonder what the point of my gift is, but sometimes I can almost see the hand guiding everything. I'm sorry you had to go through what you did, Honey, but there was a reason. It will all work out in the end."

"I know." Honey had to believe that or she would crumple and never get up. "What about the other curses? Do you know of a way I could find them? You have a lot of interesting devices in your museum."

The woman chuckled. "Yes, my husband loved to collect things, the weirder the better. I can't think of anything here that would help you, but you could try seeking."

"For a thing? How would that work?"

"You'd need something related to it, in this case another curse."

"You're saying if I find one, I should be able to find the others."

"Theoretically, yes."

"Thank you. You've been very helpful."

The old woman gave a regal nod, "and thank you for having tea with an old woman. Not too many youngsters these days would have accepted my invitation. Excellent disguise, by the way, I didn't recognize you at all."

"Thank you."

"Now, off you go. Come see me again when you are famous rather than infamous."

"Ha ha."

8

HONEY – AUGUST 16 – ROME

The bright sunshine nearly blinded her when Honey stepped out of the museum. She quickly exchanged her frames for her sunglasses with taps from the appropriate fingers then turned to her right and tried to walk calmly. Only the skirt she was wearing prevented her from doing a couple of cartwheels down the bright sidewalk. She finally had a place to start! There couldn't be that many old stone circles in the world, could there? In fact, the only one she knew of was Stonehenge. Could it be that easy? All she had to do was go to the UK, retrieve Mr. No-Name's part of the curse, and use it to find the rest. Following the directions the girl at the front desk of the museum had shared, Honey made her way to a human library complete with public computers to do some research.

To her utter lack of surprise, there were, in fact, many stone circles in the UK and Ireland, perhaps hundreds. Stonehenge was one of the most preserved, but its stones were too big to be from the vision, and she didn't remember any capping stones. She spent the next several hours zooming into Google Maps to look at all the stone circles, which were not necessarily henges, she discovered. A henge always had both a bank and a ditch but did not always have stones. Also, both the circles and stones came in many different sizes and some circles had been moved over the years.

None of the posted pictures looked right.

She sagged back in the creaky wooden chair. What other clues had been in the vision? She was pretty certain the guy had been from the UK. He spoke English and had a European-sounding accent as did all the other witches. The circle had been on a hill with a few scraggly trees around and lots of grass that disappeared in the dark edges of the vision. It was windy. The man's stringy hair had kept covering his face. In other words, the circle could be or could have been anywhere in the UK except areas populated with buildings during the time of the plague.

She thought again of that poor boy in the vision. Who was he? She was certain he'd been killed to fuel the curse, but was there a specific reason he'd been chosen? Was he a hybrid like her, or perhaps a curse-breaker? What happened if a curse-breaker's blood was used to set a curse?

That was a clue! If the place was cursed, someone would have noted it at some point. She searched for cursed places in the UK and came up with a lot of haunted sites but no curses. Interesting. Had ancient European witches not used curses as much as ancient Egyptians or had they all been broken?

She was getting side-tracked. What other clues did she have? Right, the book. She dug the old lady's book out of her backpack and opened it for the first time. The seer's handwriting was tall and thin and flowed elegantly in straight lines across paper that didn't have lines. Unfortunately, it was all in Italian.

84

Honey had been in Italy long enough to recognize days and months were written at the top of each separate section, but she couldn't decipher much beyond that. She'd have to buy a notebook and a dictionary and start translating. How long would that take her?

The lady had said she wrote down the sounds. They wouldn't be in Italian. Honey started flipping through the book, looking for anything out of the ordinary. Just past the middle, she found some letters not forming Italian-looking words, but still words, with lots of dashes in-between. Neither she nor Google could interpret them.

Her stomach reminded her with a loud, irritated growl that she hadn't eaten since early morning. Honey collected her things, then made her way through the pleasantly cool library to the entry/exit door. Outside was a sauna. Even though the sun had passed its zenith and was far enough down that one side of the street was shaded, the heat now radiated not just from the sun, but from the bricks all around and through the soles of her shoes.

She nearly went back inside the library, but then a beautiful, tomato-y, cheesy smell caressed her nose. The enticing scent lured her down a tiny street with vines trained up the wall and across ropes strung between the buildings. The restaurant she found was too small for more than a couple of tables inside, but there were several outside in the shade of the building and the overhead vines. A small fountain trickling playfully next to the restaurant door added to the illusion of coolness. She bought two pieces of pizza and the largest cold drink they carried in their tiny fridge, then sat down at one of the outside tables. She'd just taken her first bite when she smelled that imitation-wolf scent again. She'd smelled it on the way to the library too. Odd.

Her body was screaming at her to do something other than sit. If it hadn't been so hot, she would have considered running despite just eating pizza, but it *was* hot, and she only had an hour before she was supposed to work in the hostel. She promised herself she'd go for a run later, then walked to the hostel. She might as well have run as sweaty as she was by the time she reached her destination. It was time to do laundry anyway. After a very quick shower to cool down, she dumped her pillowcase full of dirty clothes in the hostel's washer.

Four hours later, her shift was over and she was folding the clean laundry when she again smelled Emmerico's scent. How was that possible? She was on the second floor and there was no one in the room, although the window was open. She peered outside. Several people were walking by below, but she didn't see Emmerico. Was she imagining things or was he following her?

Thinking of scents made her think of Brayton. No one else was in the room, so she pulled her backpack out of the nether, and dug out the slate.

Dear Wasp,
[Aug. 16, 6am] Ha ha.

She grinned. He'd liked her turtle joke.

Even better, for once she had something exciting to say. Writing as small as she could, she filled up the entire slate with a description of what she'd seen in the museum. Another girl came into the room while she was writing, but barely glanced at her. After she was done, Honey carried her backpack into the bathroom, changed into some gym attire, and then tucked her backpack safely into the nether.

Outside, the sun was only a faint glow on the horizon and the temperature had cooled enough to be almost comfortable. She turned toward the Tiber River and the nice bike path she'd discovered and set out at a steady pace.

The trail had lights, but some sections were dark sketchy. With her ability to freeze people, she wasn't too worried, but still, even she could be bested if someone had a dart gun. Was it even possible to buy one of those in Rome?

The sun was completely down by the time she turned back. She was making her way through one of the darker sections of the trail when someone emerged from the shadows to run beside her. She recognized his scent immediately.

"Emmerico?"

"Si, Signorina. I told you we'd meet again."

"No you didn't."

"You're brave to go running by yourself after dark. I admire that in a woman."

She heard the shuffle of another pair of shoes behind her and smelled, was that rope? They were trying to use a binding spell on her? Without looking, she froze Emmerico and whoever was behind her. Two more people stepped onto the path in front of her. One of them held a metal pipe. What was this, a bad 80's movie? She froze them too and ran at top speed to the stairs that led up to street level and to her hostel. A few seconds later, she crashed through the door and had to lean over to breathe.

"Good run?" She noted tanned, athletic legs and several tattoos while she raised her eyes to a set of warm, brown eyes under dark hair with curls wilder than hers. She sucked in his scent. Cologne, shaving gel, toothpaste, but no imitation wolf. Likely not one of Emmerico's friends.

"A warm one." She was so drenched in sweat it looked like she'd just come in out of the rain.

The mystery guy offered her a bottle of water. "Here. I just grabbed it from the fridge."

It wasn't opened. Maybe it was foolish, but she was so thirsty, she took it from him and downed several beautifully cool sips. "Thank you. This is perfect."

He grinned, flashing brilliantly white teeth. "Why don't you go out with us?" he waved his hand around at the people collecting in the main lobby. "We're going out for drinks."

"Thanks for the invite, but I need to get cleaned up and stick to water, I think. Maybe another time."

He wiggled his eyebrows. "I look forward to it. Maybe we could run together sometime too?"

She didn't sense any duplicity, just attraction. It was unlikely she'd end up running with him, but she answered "sure" anyway.

She kept an eye on him while he grabbed another bottle of water and joined his group of friends. He was nice. It would be interesting to see how well a human or witch, most likely human, male could do against her in a race.

Once she was certain Emmerico and his friends weren't going to charge in through the door, she grabbed two more bottled waters and a couple of cookies someone had made and trudged past the laughing people and up the stairs.

Emmerico was a problem. Why had he tried to kidnap her? Did he know what she was? She couldn't chance it. She had to leave.

First though – a shower.

The bathroom was split into two sections with showers in one half and toilets in the other. There wasn't a way to prevent people from coming in, but she didn't plan on being there long. She sent her shoes to the nether, then stepped inside with all her other clothes on. If it was as warm in the UK as it was in Rome, she wouldn't have to worry about wet clothes for long.

She lathered up and rinsed as fast as she could. It didn't take long at all with her short hair. She turned around to make sure she'd rinsed the last bit of soap off her back and noticed a shadow on the floor under her shower curtain. Before she could respond in any way, the curtain zipped open and a woman she had never seen before blew something off her palm toward her. Honey instinctively formed a shield and sent the outer layer with all the dust flying back at the woman. The woman leapt back, but not before she got a face-full of whatever it was. Honey sent her into the wall with a wet foot to the chest, then darted past her toward the bathroom door. She was prepared for someone to be waiting in the hall, but not for the black fabric that came down over her head when she cleared the last shower stall or the beefy arms that grabbed her around the waist and hoisted her up over an equally beefy shoulder. Her first instinct was to freeze whoever had her, but nothing happened. She tried to make the cloth disappear but was again thwarted. That's when she realized the net smelled like a shield. Hah. Someone thought they could keep her from using her magic with a shielded sack. Not for long. She pictured the molecules the maker had immobilized to create the spell between the weave of the fabric and blasted them apart, then froze her captor.

Instead of stopping, he tilted forward. Not wanting to be squashed like a pancake, she pulled in all the air around them to cushion her fall. It felt like the fall took an abnormally long time. She felt a jolt, then a sharp edge hit her backside and she was flying. It felt like she was in the right orientation to land on her back, but her head slammed into something and everything went black.

9

HONEY - UNKNOWN

Her head hurt.

What was that awful smell?

She turned her head far enough to sniff the fabric beneath her and shuddered. Why was she lying on something that smelled like unwashed body and urine and dirt? Where was she? She opened her eyes and a bright slice of light pierced her eyeball. Her stomach quenched and she gagged, but nothing came up.

Turning away from the light, but unfortunately into more of the awful-smelling fabric, she shaded her eyes and attempted to open them again. This time she saw a wall, a very rough wall made of pitted stone with chunks of plaster still attached. What was this place?

There were no windows. The light that had seemed so bright wasn't really that bright. She was able to look around without gagging after a minute or two. The light came from an arched doorway carved in stone. She couldn't see the light's source around a wall or whatever blocked the doorway further in, but the light wasn't steady so perhaps a candle or a fire?

Why did her head hurt so much?

Maybe she was dehydrated. Her mouth was so dry she doubted she could make spit. She needed water. A deep sniff clear of the smelly blankets informed her there was some close by somewhere.

She pushed the material covering her body away. Cool air bathed her bare skin and immediately stole all the warmth remaining from the nasty blanket. Why had she gone to sleep in her running clothes?

Her head and shoulders and backside protested painfully as she rolled onto her hands and knees. Her stomach didn't feel all that great either. After the nausea passed, she gingerly felt the side of her head where it hurt the worst. Her hair was stiff and crinkly and covered with, she sniffed the nearly black powder now coating her fingers, blood. Lovely. She'd hit her head, but how had she gotten here? Where was here? Ugh, her mouth felt like she'd been eating dirt. Where was the water?

Tiny pebbles dug into her palms and knees as she crawled across the stone floor to the source of the water smell – a stone bowl in the corner where a thin stream of water was trickling from a hole in the wall. The bowl was discolored with either growth or minerals or both, but the water itself smelled good. She opened her mouth under the trickle and drank until she was satisfied.

The trickle was so small she really couldn't drink that much, but when she pulled away, her stomach rebelled violently. She heaved and spewed all the liquid that had made it to her stomach all over the floor. The violent motion made her head spin even more. She sank against the wall next to the puddle and concentrated on not moving. Eventually the world stopped spinning and the nauseous feeling subsided, leaving her thirsty again. Cautiously and slowly, she took only a few sips, then waited several minutes against the wall before taking a few more.

The room she was in wasn't big. Other than the pile of bedding on the floor against the longest wall and the little fountain, there was nothing else in the room, not even on the deep shelves dug into the wall above the bedding. The place in general felt large though. Somewhere through the arched doorway she could hear voices, but they were hollow and distorted like they'd bounced around for a while. The cadence was familiar, but the words themselves were mostly incomprehensible. What language was it, Spanish? No. Italian, it was Italian.

Why was she in a place where people spoke Italian?

All right, what did she know? She was in….um…she was from…hmm…a place with trees and green fields and warm days and snow and it was shaped like a pointy rectangle but the name escaped her. This wasn't it though, she knew that. She was a…she looked down at herself… runner. Yep, those were running clothes and she had a tan on her legs that stopped at her ankles, so she ran outside. Okay, and she could do things. She twitched her finger and a scruffy-looking backpack popped out of nowhere. She unzipped the front pocket and pulled out the bar she'd known was there. Food was good. She needed food. What else was in there? A passport for someone named Penny Velos. She didn't recognize the name, but the picture was familiar. What else: a passport for someone named Isabelle Winters. The pictures were very similar. Huh. She had more than one ID and more than one name. No wonder she couldn't remember what her name was. Why did she have more than one name. That wasn't normal, was it?

She dug deeper and pulled out some plastic cards with dollar amounts written on them and a piece of cardboard with a big green happy face at the top with a patch over one eye. It was important, but she couldn't remember why. Someone had written on it.

Dear Wasp. [Aug 16, 10 pm]. Wow. Send me some of the words and I'll try to identify them too. Be safe.

Dear Wasp. [Aug 17, 11 pm]. You there? I'm supposed to meet with your Gma again tomorrow.

[Aug 18, 4 am] Did you turn your phone off again? Please tell me you're okay.

Her name was Wasp? She liked it. She looked at her watch, or where it should be. There was a tan line there, but no watch.

Hi. I don't know the time or day. I bumped my head. I don't know where I am. I must have lost my phone. My watch is gone too. I'm in a stone building in my running clothes and I can hear people speaking Italian, I think. I'm okay. I found food in my bag. Do you know where I am?

Should she ask who she was speaking to?

Someone was coming. She hastily stuffed everything back into her backpack and put it back into the…the nothing? That didn't sound right. She wrapped her arms around her knees for warmth and watched the doorway.

She automatically took a long sniff when a young man walked through the door. He smelled familiar, maybe.

His eyes were on the bedding and not the rest of the room. She could have snuck out behind him if she'd thought her head would allow it.

It wouldn't.

He came to a sudden stop, like she'd frozen him. Could she freeze people? It felt like she could. She hadn't froze him though since he was now turning slowly in a circle. It looked like he was searching more with his nose than his eyes. He started a little when he spotted her, then smiled. He had a nice smile.

"You're awake. I'm surprised. That was a nasty fall."

"What happened?"

"What do you remember?"

He might have a nice smile, but something told her not to trust him. She really wished she could remember why.

"It doesn't matter what I remember. I want to hear your side of the story."

"You want to know why we tried to capture you on the path and why we kidnapped you."

He did what now? This was bad. She should freeze him and run, but maybe not right now. She closed her eyes at yet another surge of nausea threatened to make her lose the water she'd managed to imbibe.

"Stai bene?"

She wasn't sure what that meant. She kept her eyes closed and hoped the nausea would pass uneventfully. It did, eventually. When she opened her eyes again, the young man was squatting in front of her.

"We didn't mean to hurt you. We only want your help. All you have to do is call your mom or dad, have them send some funds, and we'll get you to the nearest healer."

"My help?"

"Yeah." He rubbed his thumb against his finger. "Your monetary help."

An immense sorrow weighed her down, but why, she didn't know. That, on top of the pain in her head, was enough to cause tears to leak out her eyes. The tears made her head hurt worse. She put her forehead down on her knees.

"Don't cry. Just pull your phone out of wherever you stashed it and call someone, then we'll let you go."

She lifted her head slowly so she could watch him. "Stashed it? What do you mean?"

He snorted. "Don't play dumb. I saw you do it."

"You saw me with a phone?"

He rolled his eyes. "No, a bag. You had a bag one moment and the next you didn't."

"Where was I when you saw this?"

"At the hostel, in the laundry room."

Okay, she was staying in a hostel and doing laundry. Why was she at a hostel? Was she traveling? She wouldn't have pulled things out of the nothing with him watching. Humans might see. Humans? Right. She wasn't human and neither was he.

"You were spying on me."

He shrugged, "Yeah."

She couldn't remember the hostel at all, but maybe she'd learn more if she kept him talking. "How?"

"There was a tree outside the window and I'm a very good climber." He stretched out his fingers to show claws that quickly disappeared. The claws didn't really surprise her, but his smell did. He didn't smell right.

"What are you?"

He shook his head. "It doesn't matter. Pull out your phone and call your folks."

"I don't think…" A fire and two bodies flashed into her mind. "Mom," she whispered before the pain in her head became too great and she passed out again.

10

HONEY – UNKNOWN – LATER

Voices woke her. Someone had wrapped her in the nasty blankets again, but over their stench she caught the rich scent of pepperoni. Her mouth salivated painfully. At the same time, she wanted to cry. Why? The memory was right there. What was it? She'd been hungry just like she was now and…No, she was hungrier now. She hadn't eaten in… she couldn't remember. Where was the pizza? She needed it *now*.

"You done?" a female voice demanded.

Honey blinked. A mostly empty pizza box was in front of her. Her belly felt painfully full, and her face felt greasy. She wiped her mouth with the back of her hand. Really greasy. She pushed the box away toward the young woman glaring down at her. Behind the woman, two young men were sitting on the floor, one holding his nose and glaring and the other dabbing at some scratches on his arm. The one with the scratches looked vaguely familiar.

"What happened?"

"What do you mean what happened?" the woman snarled.

She nodded to the injured men. "To them."

"You attacked them."

"I did?" She didn't remember doing that, but for some reason she wasn't surprised either.

"You growled at us. Are you a wolf or a shifter?" the man with the bloody nose asked behind his hand.

"A shifter?"

"Don't play numb."

"Numb?"

"I thought you said she was a witch," the woman said.

"I thought she was," the guy with the scratches replied. "She doesn't smell like a shifter, and she could see the witch museum."

She sniffed her arm. It smelled like the awful blanket she was sitting on. "What do shifters smell like?"

The one with the scratches stood and approached her. He was starting to look familiar. He lifted his lower arm toward her nose. "Like me."

"Emm, don't!" the woman said.

The man, Emm leaned a little closer. Honey leaned forward and took a deep sniff. He smelled of dust and sun and sweat, but beneath that there was a musky scent she couldn't place even though she was pretty sure she'd smelled it before. It wasn't quite wolf. Keeping her eyes on him, she straightened so that her back was against the wall. He gave a little smile and squatted in front of her. He didn't look dangerous, but something told her to be wary.

"What is your name?"

"Name?"

"Yes. What do people call you?" he asked kindly.

"What people?"

"Your family. Your friends."

Friends? Did she have friends? She did. The best of friends, but they were far away and she didn't know when she'd ever get to see them again. She was lonely, so lonely. Like a wave, the feeling overwhelmed her and she was caught in its flood. She covered her face while the sobs wracked her body. The wave of grief disappeared almost as fast as it had come, but it reminded her how bad her head had hurt before and how thirsty she'd been. There was something in her eye too. She rubbed it out, then inspected whatever it was. It was brown and round. She touched her other eye and a second one came out. Gross. She wiped them on her shorts.

The guy had moved closer and was rubbing his hand over her nearly bare back, muttering things she didn't understand. She wiped her eyes one more time, then looked up at him. "What are you saying?"

His eyes widened and his hand moved to cup her cheek. "Bellissima."

She might not know her name or where she was, but a strange guy touching her was not normal. She knocked his arm away. "No touching."

He put his hands in the air, palms up. "Sorry, Bellissima. I could not help myself. Your eyes. I've never seen such beautiful emeralds. Why would you cover them?"

"Knock it off Emmerico," the woman said. "We don't have time for this. We need her name."

"Why do you need my name?" Keeping her senses attuned to the guy beside her, she turned her head enough to monitor the two other people in the room.

"You don't remember?" Emmerico asked.

She searched her mind. She remembered now that she'd talked to the guy before, but couldn't recall what they'd said. "No."

"Do you remember your name?"

"No."

"Merda." the woman grumbled and kicked the man still squatting on the floor in front of Honey, "This is all your fault."

Emmerico moved suddenly and grabbed her hands. "Bellissima, are you sure? Try to remember. We cannot help you if you cannot tell us your name."

She jerked her hands out of his and shoved his chest. She only meant to push him away but he skidded back several feet before he landed on his rear under the archway. He looked more surprised than hurt. Good.

"I said, no touching."

The woman snorted.

The man with the bloody nose shook his head at the one on the floor. "I don't think she likes men."

"Why is that the first conclusion you make when a girl says no?" the woman asked, shaking her head at the both of them. Looking back at Honey, she said, "Ragazza, I want to take a look at your head where you fell. Will you let me?"

Honey reached up and touched her head. Her hair was still crusty but her skin wasn't sensitive to the touch and she didn't feel any cut. "I'm fine. How did I hit my head?"

"You fell," the woman said shortly, cutting off Emmerico who had picked himself up to stand behind the woman again.

"How?"

In her mind's eye, Honey saw the woman blow something at her and then fall against a wall. She tried to hold on to the memory, to see what happened, but all she could remember after that was blackness.

"It was an accident," the woman answered.

These people weren't friends, otherwise they would know her name and wouldn't blow dust at her. "Why didn't you take me to the hospital after I fell?"

The woman opened her lips, frowned, then closed her mouth. Emmerico stepped around her and started speaking before the woman could try again.

"We are shifters, Bellissima. Human hospitals are not for our kind. Also, our friend was injured as well and we were distracted by his care."

Something in his face told her the answer but she asked anyway. "How is he?"

"He is still sleeping."

"And that's not normal for a shifter?" she inquired.

"No."

"We heal much faster than humans," the woman added.

"How did he get injured?"

"Just spit it out you two," the man with the nose grumbled. "We kidnapped you. You and Fazio fell down the stairs and hit your heads. We'll let you go as soon as someone pays your ransom."

"Ransom?" To her surprise, she was relieved. They didn't know…what was it? Her brain helpfully showed her random images of a fire, then an older guy leering down at her with lots of charms around his neck, then a boy, no boys, four of them, smiling and laughing with her, and fifth, scowling. Then he was smiling and swinging her around.

"Ragazza, what's wrong with you?" the woman asked.

"I'm remembering," she mumbled.

"What do you remember?" Emmerico asked, sitting in front of her, but far enough that she'd have to lunge to push him over.

There were so many images. "I don't know."

"Focus. Do you remember who your parents are? Do you remember their names, their numbers?"

A woman smiled. A handsome man with brown hair curling out from under his hat picked them both up in one huge hug, then there was fire. The world in her head collapsed but somehow she didn't.

"It wouldn't do any good. They're dead." She swiped at the tears, but they just kept coming.

"Brothers, sisters, aunts, uncles, grandparents, cousins?"

An image of a young man with a little boy surrounded by older kids and women popped up. There was the glowing shape of a woman and another fire. The grumpy boy was burned, badly. She was scared. There was an older lady with a nice smile and white hair. With the back of her hand, Honey lightly brushed the bottom of her sports bra where she'd pinned the charm the old lady had given her…her grandmother? Still there. What did it do though? Something about wolves. The scene switched to another fire, but this one was surrounded by a circle of girls who were chatting and laughing and spouting magic. Witches, and she was one of them, but she'd left. She'd run.

"Did you remember someone?" Emmerico's voice queried hopefully.

"I'm alone." Technically true.

"You're a runaway?"

That sounded oddly right. "Yes."

She stank of smoke and sweat and dirt and was standing in line with a lot of older people, then she was running through a parking garage. Someone was whistling. She knew him. Why was she running away? No, she didn't know him then. She knew him now.

"You're not poor though," Emmerico was saying. "You paid for that overpriced water and spent all day in the library and the museum. If you were truly a runaway you wouldn't have the time or money for that."

She was wiping tables and talking to a couple of little kids.

"I had a job."

"Must be easy when you're all cute and innocent-looking," the woman groused. "I knew this wasn't going to work."

"What wasn't going to work? Why do you need ransom money?" Honey asked.

The man with the nose stood. The bottom part of his face was covered with blood, but he walked closer like there was nothing wrong. He was about the same age as Emmerico, but thicker and taller. "Because this doesn't come for free."

"This what?" Honey asked.

He waved his hands around at the crumbling stone walls, "This home, this life, this territory, doesn't come for free. We must pay our dues."

She suspected he was about to do something she wouldn't like, but she chose to pretend naivete and glance around. "Where are we?"

"Wouldn't you like to know." The bloody man lunged at her and she felt something sharper than his fingernail poke her underneath the chin. "And if you don't provide a name and the number of someone who can pay your $10,000 ransom, this will be your final resting place. Also, in case you're wondering why your magic doesn't work, we fitted you with an inhibitor collar while you were sleeping."

She touched her neck. There was something hard and thin there, but it was easy to send it to the nether. She froze the nose guy's limbs so he could still hear her but wouldn't be able to stab her and moved away from his claw.

"You mean this," Honey said, pulling the round thing back out of the nether once her hand was clear of her neck. It didn't smell like an inhibitor or a shield or even a binding smell. She brought it to her nose for a better sniff.

"Told you she was a witch," Emmerico smirked.

"It's not an inhibitor," Honey said, sniffing at it again. "I don't sense any magic at all."

"It's magic. It is definitely magic," Emmerico insisted. "Annia wouldn't lie."

"Annia, the girl you've jilted how many times?" the woman scoffed.

"Annia knows what I am. She knows I'm not one for attachments."

Honey turned on the ability to see molecules that she'd just remembered she had and held the round thing up so she could keep an eye on her two non-frozen captors while she inspected it. Nose guy was glaring at her, but she'd frozen his mouth so he couldn't say a word. There were molecules doing something in the necklace, but it was in a very tight, confined part.

"There's a battery." What an odd word. It was the right one though, perhaps.

"A battery?"

The woman snatched the necklace from Honey and inspected it herself.

"Merda! It's a tracker. Emmerico, you idiot, you brought a tracker down here. Now Gaio will know where we are."

Emmerico snatched it from her and looked it over himself. After a moment he shrugged and offered it back. "She won't find us. We're underground. I doubt it can send a signal from here. We've had it since Saturday and nothing has happened."

They were underground? That explained the chill and the musty smell and the lack of windows.

The woman jerked it from his hands and flared her nose at him. "She's biding her time."

"Who's Gaio?" Honey asked.

"Funny you should ask," a sultry voice said from somewhere on the other side of the arch. A moment later, a slim yet curvy, dark-haired beauty with deep brown eyes and eyelashes so thick and long Honey was almost certain they weren't real, stepped into view.

"You're Gaio?"

"Tuh," the girl huffed. "This is the kind of girl you prefer over me, Emmy?"

"No, of course not," Emmerico said, spinning to face the newcomer and reaching for her hands. "She's going to make us lots of money."

The girl looked Honey up and down. "You going to pimp her out? I don't think you'll get much."

"No, no. She's rich. We're waiting on her ransom."

The woman raised an elegant eyebrow. "Someone is going to pay ransom for a streetwalker? Did you steal her from a rich pimp?"

"She's not a streetwalker. We nabbed her while she was in the shower."

The woman's nose wrinkled. "You should have waited until she was done. She reeks."

"Why are you here Annia?" the other woman asked.

Annia shrugged. "I wanted to see this 'perfect lair' that Emmy was bragging about. I'm not impressed."

"Are you going to tell your mother?" the other woman demanded.

"I haven't decided yet." Her eyes fell on the man Honey had frozen. "What's wrong with Arrigo? Why is he just crouching there?"

Honey scooted out of the way while Annia walked around Arrigo to look at his face. He'd start to thaw in a few more seconds. Should she refreeze him?

"He's…" Emmerico began.

"practicing," the other woman interrupted.

"For what?" Annia asked, poking the smooth part of one of Arrigo's cheeks, not once, but twice. The second time, he abruptly turned and chomped his teeth at her finger. Annia jerked away and gave him a scathing glare.

"Doesn't he make a good statue? All we have to do is get him a toga and paint him gray."

Annia gave a feminine snort. "Why bother with a toga? I'm sure his … assets, or lack of them, will help him blend right in."

Arrigo growled.

Annia laughed and patted him on the head right before he straightened and sent a mean look Honey's way.

"Now you," Annia crouched down to look Honey in the face but kept her distance. Her lip curled like she was near a dung heap. Honey didn't blame her. "You're pretty enough we probably could get something for you if we cleaned you up, but you've got useful skills too. How would you like a job?"

Annia smelled like a straight-up wolf. No imitation-flavoring for her. There was a faint green glow all around her though. Honey shot a quick glance at Emmerico. He had it too, but his was tinged with yellow. She could see magic? Right, she could. She focused back on Annia who was still crouched in front of her, waiting expectantly.

"What kind of a job?"

"Acquisition and retrieval."

"No!" the other woman protested. "This is our lair, our territory, our witch. Go back to your fancy villa and leave us alone."

Annia rose gracefully to face the other woman, but Honey noted she'd placed herself so she could keep everyone in view. "Carmy, Carmy, Carmy,"

"Carmela!"

Annia gave the tiniest of shrugs, "Technically everything belongs to the Claw. You know that. If you want to show that you are worthy of," she waved at the rough walls around them, "this, you must show you can turn a profit. I'm just trying to help you use your resources wisely."

"No you're not. You see we have something good and you're taking it for yourself."

Annia gave another tiny shrug. "Mamma said I should take an interest. You clearly need my help. It's a win-win."

"For whom!?"

Emmerico dropped a hand on Carmela's shoulder. "Let's hear her out, Cam. What did you have in mind Annia?"

Honey couldn't see the look Carmela gave him, but Emmerico hastily removed his hand and stepped back.

"You are all skilled, but with her help," Annia nodded at Honey, "you could take it to the next level."

"You don't think we know that?"

"No. Based on Arrigo's bloody face and Emme's arm, she can fight, and I saw the tracker disappear for a moment. What else can she do?"

"Run and eat and stink," Arrigo offered.

Annia looked down at Honey. "What is your name?"

Several names flitted through her thoughts – Isabella, Penny, Frederica, Madeline – but none of them felt right.

"I don't know."

"You will be Mal then."

"Mal?" Carmela asked.

"For Malodorous. Clean her up. We'll test her skills tonight. Dress her in something boring. Oh, and here," Annia squatted in front of Honey.

In an impressive burst of speed, the young woman abruptly grabbed Honey's wrist and snapped something around it. Honey jerked her arm back, but it was already too late – the band was locked onto her wrist. It even had a small keyhole.

"It's an inhibitor. Behave and I'll remove it tonight."

11

HONEY – AUGUST SOMETHING – MUCH LATER

Honey stopped and rested her hand against the rough-cut wall before she closed her eyes. The smell was different, but she'd been in a tunnel like this before, recently. She'd been wearing a lot of makeup and was running from something. It had something to do with a library. Why had she been running from a library?

"Keep moving." Carmela urged ahead of her.

"I was remembering something."

"Remember later."

"Maybe it's from when we carried you down here," Emmerico suggested behind her.

"Maybe." It wasn't though. She didn't remember being carried at all except right before she fell.

The end of the tunnel was now close enough that she could see the light ahead was coming from yet another, much wider tunnel. Carmela ducked under the rope blocking their tunnel from the bigger one and disappeared. Emmerico grabbed Honey's arm before she could step into the light and pulled her back against the wall. Within a minute, Carmela was back.

"It's all clear. The cleaning lady is gone. Come."

Honey followed Carmela up some stone stairs into a much nicer room with tiled floors and walls constructed of of laid stone instead of carved-out of stone. Ancient art covered much of the wall surface. Folded, colorful pamphlets in a rack by the door suggested it was popular with tourists.

"Where are we?"

"Don't worry about it. Here," she pulled open a heavy wooden door. "Wash your hair in the sink, take off your clothes and throw them away, then wipe off the rest of you. I have more clothes here." She indicated the bag she was carrying.

Honey tried to take the bag of clean ones, but Carmela jerked them away.

"Clean up first."

The sink was too small to fit her head under the faucet. It took forever for her to splash enough water over her head to remove all the old blood in her hair. She did feel better though after she'd rubbed hand soap all over herself and rinsed and wiped it off with a handful of paper towels.

"Can I have the clothes now?" she asked Carmela who'd been leaning on the wall by the door and scrolling on her phone the entire time.

Carmela glanced up then went back to her phone. "Get rid of the old ones first."

"I'll change in a stall."

"Take off your clothes."

Honey crossed her arms. "Why do you want to see me naked?"

Carmela snorted. "I don't care what you look like. I'm just tired of smelling you."

"I don't smell."

Carmela pushed off the wall and walked around Honey, sniffing. "Yeah, you do."

"Well, you should have given me a clean blanket."

"You're lucky we gave you one at all." She shoved the bag of clothes at Honey. "Just take them off and put on these clean ones. I think it's worse since you got wet."

Honey took the bag and slipped into a stall. She pulled off her running top and sniffed it. Carmela was right, it didn't smell good, but no worse than that blanket. The pretty charm pinned inside her top, on the other hand, smelled like a wool cloak and…deception. Why? Why was she wearing it? She wrapped her fingers around the warm metal and closed her eyes. There was that man again, who made fire, then a glowing, woven fence, then some dogs barking, and an ugly car. Not helpful. She opened her eyes to study the magic by sight. Why was the hairband on her wrist glowing with so many colors and why, she inspected the charm in her hand, was she wearing a charm that coated her skin with a flaky blue layer of magic. The inhibitor that Annia had snapped around her wrist, on the other hand, was black – powerless, likely thanks to the second hairband right next to it with the heart-shaped charm that Honey recognized as a shield charm.

There was something about that charm, about all of them…they were for protection, to keep her safe. From what though? She flipped her wrist over to study the charm in her hand and noticed a few flakes of blue fly off her skin. Was that what Carmela was smelling? Honey pulled air molecules to her skin to trap the ones the charm was releasing and was abruptly overwhelmed with an extreme feeling of Déjà vu. She grabbed the top of the stall to keep from falling over.

"What are you doing?" Carmela asked.

"Remembering."

"Remembering what?"

"Using my magic."

"We don't have time for that. You can remember later. Annia doesn't like to wait."

"I thought you didn't like her," Honey said, pulling her backpack from the..never? She hadn't dreamed it. She really did have a backpack full of supplies. She stuffed her smelly running top inside and pulled on a clean bra.

"I never said that."

"You didn't have to."

"She's fine. Are you done yet?"

"No."

"Well, hurry up!"

Honey rolled her eyes, but quickly tugged on the cutoffs and the light blue T-shirt Carmela had supplied. The shorts were a little big, but not so much they would fall off.

"Where are we going again?" Honey asked a minute later while Carmela sniffed at her outside the stall door.

"For the twentieth time, you'll find out when we get there. You smell much better. Come on. Arrigo is waiting with the car."

It wasn't a car. It was a tiny work truck usually used by groundskeepers. Under normal circumstances it would probably be fun to ride in. Unfortunately, she had to cram into the front seat with Arrigo who did not know how to properly drive a stick and did not appreciate being told how to. Worse, the passenger door wouldn't open, and just when she'd decided to make the whole thing vanish at the next stop and make her escape, the truck pulled into a side road where a van, Annia, and two strangers were waiting.

Annia grabbed the outside handle and with a firm jerk, opened Honey's door. Before Honey could scoot away, Annia grabbed her elbow and pulled her out, then took a sniff.

"Better." She sniffed again and frowned at her. "Now you don't smell like anything."

"Must have been unscented soap."

"Whatever. Get in." She dragged Honey to the van and pushed her into the back. Emmerico, Carmela, and two strangers climbed in after her.

"Will you tell me where we're going now?" Honey asked Carmela.

"For the hundredth time, no!"

"It was only twenty the last time I asked."

Carmela huffed at her, then turned away to look out the very heavily tinted windows. They were so dark, Honey hadn't realized they were windows until after they'd climbed in the van.

The two new people smelled like imitation wolves. They clearly weren't wolves though. Wolves crammed in a van would have been just that – crammed right up next to each other, and they wouldn't have minded one bit. These people carefully kept space between them, even when the van hit a bump. Like her other companions, they were all dressed in dark clothes but didn't appear to be armed. After her question, nobody talked.

They couldn't have gone more than a mile or two before the van stopped and the back door opened.

Carmela dragged Honey out of the van to what was either a road or the start of a long driveway. One of the new people silently closed the van doors and Arrigo drove off. There weren't any stoplights along the narrow two-lane road, but with the nearly full moon, they weren't needed.

"Why are we here?" Honey asked.

"This is your job interview," Annia said looking down her nose at her, "You do a good job, you get to stay with us. You do a bad one, you will be sold to the highest bidder."

She could freeze them and run, but where would she go? She couldn't even see the next house and she suspected whatever these people changed into was faster than she was, plus they hadn't given her any shoes. What were the chances she'd stashed some rope to tie people up or maybe a dart gun?

"You can try to run if you want," Annia said, "but you won't get far and you will regret it."

"What do you want me to do?"

"Let's get off the street first."

Annia led them off the pavement and onto the gently curving cobblestone driveway. It took several minutes of walking before what Honey could only describe as a Roman villa came into view. It covered the top of the low hill and was at least two stories tall with pale, cream-colored stone that glowed faintly in the moonlight. Decorative lights luminesced under the eaves but except for one window on the second floor, everything else was dark. A long porch stretched across the front and extended out over the circular drive so people could park beneath it and go directly inside just like at a hotel. It was undoubtedly a very expensive piece of property especially this close to Rome.

Was that where she was? Rome?

Annia led them under a tree so that they were shaded from the moonlight but could still see the house. "This is the job, Mal."

"What is?"

"Inside this house, no doubt guarded with all the alarms humans can buy, are some very rare, very magical items. The problem is, the owner is human and has no idea that the items he owns can cause him harm. Your job is it get us safely in and out so we can recover the items without setting off any alarms."

That was not what she had expected. Sure, Honey had assumed they wanted to rob the place, but not for altruistic motives.

"My magic doesn't turn off alarms."

"No, but you can freeze guards and make obstacles like doors disappear, can't you?"

"Perhaps."

Annia's hand shot out and smacked Honey on the cheek so fast she didn't see it coming.

"Can you or can't you make things disappear?"

Honey's first thought was to hit her back, but then the memories came. She'd been slapped before, and hit, and kicked, but she knew how to defend herself. Her dad, her wonderful, always jovial, protective dad, had signed her up for all kinds of classes. Her beautiful, gentle, brilliant mother had too, but the classes her mother chose were tamer, like gymnastics, which she'd been good at, and art, at which she wasn't so good. She'd trained in MMA hard last year, particularly with the alpha's son, Brayton, the boy who'd burned. He'd survived though, except for his eye.

"Hey! Wake up. Snap out of it!"

She pushed back the memories to find herself backed against the trunk of a tree with Carmela's hands on her shoulders. Honey put her hand over Carmela's and gently squeezed.

"I'm good. Just remembering."

"Remember your name yet?" Annia demanded.

"No."

"Maybe I should slap you again."

"Maybe we should try this another day," Carmela said before Honey could respond. "She hit her head pretty hard and was unconscious all day yesterday. I'm surprised she's walking around. We might get caught if she has another episode at a bad time."

"No." Annia stated firmly. "The owner is coming back tomorrow. This is our only opportunity. Besides, it doesn't matter if she gets caught. She's disposable."

"She will tell them about us."

Annia focused her fierce glare on Honey. "If she gets left behind, she won't be telling anyone anything."

The girl didn't have an altruistic bone in her body.

"What else are you going to steal?" Honey asked.

"Whatever I can get my hands on."

She was honest at least.

Annia pulled a small, velvet, drawstring bag out of her pocket and dumped the contents into her hand. The moist smell of fog mixed with a pinch of magic diffused through the dry summer night air. Annia proceeded to hand out X-shaped charms to everyone but Honey.

"Don't I get one?"

"No."

"You want me to be caught on camera?" Why did that make her feel so anxious?

"How did you know what they were for?" Annia asked suspiciously.

"It was a guess," Honey admitted, although she was pretty sure they were obscuring charms. How she knew was another mystery.

"You don't need to worry about the cameras. They're taken care of." Annia tapped a big black watch on her wrist.

No way was she trusting whatever that watch was. She couldn't detect any magic from it at all. She did however detect several charms on Annia and the two people she'd brought, including protection charms and a two death charms. She disabled the death charms. No one was getting killed if she could help it.

"Now let me have your arm and I'll remove the inhibitor. Don't try anything though. My friends and I are wearing protection charms. Your magic won't work on us."

So that's why they had them. Honey focused on the charms while Annia unlocked the bracelet. She disabled them just in time to see Annia stab a syringe in her lower arm. She froze whatever liquid was in the syringe along with Annia's body and her own arm. Then for good measure, she froze everyone around.

Honey unfroze Annia's thumb so she could pull back the plunger a little before backing away from the syringe. It was one of the biggest needles she'd even seen. "What did you try to inject me with?"

"Poison," Annia spat. "You'll die even with that little bit if you don't get the antidote and that is in the van. I'm not calling the van until we're done."

"What kind of poison?"

"I'm not going to tell you."

Honey did her best to push out any liquid that might have come from the syringe out of her body, then sniffed at her arm. It smelled like blood. She slipped the syringe out of Annia's hand and sniffed at the tip of the needle. It smelled like salt. Was it just a saline solution? Annia didn't smell like she was bluffing, but then people didn't smell like they were lying if they thought they were telling the truth.

There was one surefire way to get Annia to call the van early. She emptied the syringe into Annia's arm.

Annia started cussing, or perhaps calling her names. Honey couldn't understand anything since it was all in Italian.

"Shall I call the van now?"

Annia's nose elongated and the long, dark hair on top of her head shrank at the same time more dark hair spread over her face. Honey had seen someone transform before, but she was pretty sure it had never been into a cat. Annia's nose was too big to belong to a house cat, and she certainly wasn't the size of one. A panther perhaps?

Annia's limbs were still frozen except for where Honey had thawed her arm to inject the syringe. Honey suspected that was the only reason she didn't have a fully transformed panther at her throat. To be safe, she froze Annia's limbs again before thawing Carmela's head.

"So, that happened." Honey nodded at Annia. "Are you all cats?"

Carmela's jaw fell. "Dio santo! What did you do?"

"I injected that syringe of stuff into her. She got mad. Was it truly poison?"

"I don't know. I don't know what it is. Bacco or Romeo might know."

"Seriously, his name is Romeo?" Why did that amuse her so much?

Honey refroze everyone's limbs and then unfroze everyone's heads.

"How did you freeze them?" Carmela asked over Annia's hissing and growling as the others became aware of their predicament. "They had protection charms."

Honey lifted her wrist to show the heart-shaped one dangling off the hairband they'd never bothered to remove from her when she was unconscious. "They're my specialty. If I can make them, I can break them."

"If you want the antidote, you better release us," one of the extras snarled.

"Was it truly a poison then?"

"Release us or you'll find out the hard way."

"You mean Annia will find out the hard way, because I injected most of it into her."

"You did what!"

It was probably a good thing she couldn't understand what he was saying.

"How do I call the van?" she asked the other, quieter one.

"Unfreeze me and I'll do it."

"Right. No."

Honey froze their limbs again and started searching. She found his cell phone in his front pocket and pressed his frozen thumb onto the screen to open it. Arrigo's name wasn't in the list of contacts and the man stubbornly refused to tell her which one it was. She did recognize one of the names though.

Was calling her the smart move? No matter who she called, she wouldn't have much time to get away, especially if they all transformed into cats after they thawed. Another memory popped into her head, a useful one this time. She quickly walked up to each of them and visualized what she wanted, ending in front of Carmela.

"What are you doing?"

"I'll explain in a moment." Honey tapped the phone and made the call. A woman with a sharp voice answered it after only two rings.

"Hello. Is this Gaio?" Honey asked.

Everyone's eyes grew wide, including Annia's.

"I am. Who is this?"

"I can't remember, but I thought you'd like to know that Annia tried to inject me with poison and I stole the syringe from her and injected it into her arm instead. She says there's an antidote in the van but I don't know how to contact the van. Was it truly a poison? If so, I apologize. I thought she was bluffing."

"Where is she?"

"I don't know where we are. She was planning to rob a big house. Do you know what was in the syringe? Should I apply some kind of first aid?"

"What did it look like?"

"A clear solution. It smelled like salt."

"How much did you inject?"

"All of it."

Annia wasn't the only one in her family who could cuss. Honey dropped the phone at Carmela's feet. She hoped, for Annia's sake, the antidote worked and for her own, that the poison wasn't deadly. She felt fine so far.

"I'm leaving. I have bound your powers so you can't transform to chase me, but you can unlock them yourselves. You just have to sing the lyrics to a certain pop song."

"What pop song?"

"I'll leave a clue for you somewhere."

"Wait, per favore," Carmela said. "You can't tell anyone about us. No one knows we exist."

"Why?"

"It's forbidden."

"Why?"

"I can't say. Just trust me."

"Okay. I won't tell, I promise, as long as you don't kidnap anyone else or sell them into slavery, or anything like that."

Carmela nodded. Honey sent the syringe to…whatever it was called, refroze everyone completely, and started down the drive.

She needed some shoes, or wait a second, she remembered feeling the wind in the fur on her back. She could transform too. A moment later, she had four feet. She jumped over the fence along the side of the drive and ran full-out toward the lights on the horizon. With every step, more memories surfaced. She had friends, lots of friends, but four best friends – Nathan, Luke, Liam, and Walter. They were wolves too and they knew what she was long before anyone else. She remembered the librarian and several libraries and Canada and finally, just as she reached a place where the dirt roads abruptly became narrow, crowded paved ones, she remembered why it was so hard to remember her name.

It wasn't safe to stay as a wolf, nor was it safe to enter the city, not if the cat pack was prowling for her. Gaio would undoubtedly order a full-scale hunt for her after she retrieved her daughter. The cats would be branching out in all directions from where she started and likely checking all the major roads, assuming there were enough of them. How and why had a cat pack stayed hidden? Were there other animals people could transform into?

It was a mystery for another day. She had to leave.

Honey stopped inside the crumbling corner of an old building and quickly exchanged the borrowed clothes for her own. After hastily jotting the name of the song onto a piece of paper from the back of her notebook, she tucked the paper into the pocket of the borrowed cutoffs and laid them on top of the wall. Assuming a homeless person didn't take them, the cats would find them, otherwise Annia might be stuck with a cat head and human body. Hmm – once she got her powers back would Annia be able to go all human or all cat again or would she always be mixed? Yet another mystery. Honey pulled the shell she'd finally remembered existed into the palm of her hand, pictured the only circle of stones that was clear in her memory, and stepped into the wall.

12

BRAYTON – AUGUST 19 – INDIANA

"Brayton, you're here early."

He jumped and turned midair to face the librarian who'd snuck up behind him again. How did she always manage to do that?

"I had another errand but it didn't take as long as I thought it would," he lied.

"Lucky for you, Mrs. Wixx is early too. Come on, she's waiting in my office."

Ms. Carrier's office smelled of magic, but it didn't reek. Ms. Carrier herself though was another story. He held his breath while he followed her into the dim hallway where the offices were.

Rachel Wixx wiggled her eyebrows at him over a cup of steaming tea when he walked in. She'd asked him to call her Rachel, but it felt odd.

"Good afternoon, Mrs. Wixx."

"Good afternoon, Mr. Mooney. Would you like a cup of tea?"

"No thank you." He had to get her alone. "I, ah, thought I'd take you out for coffee today."

"Coffee? The kind with all the milk in it?"

"You mean a latte?"

"Yes, that," Mrs. Wixx grinned. "I would love to go out on a date with you, young man, but first, let me look at that eye. Oh, and before I forget, I made cookies. They came out a bit dry, unfortunately."

He ignored the date comment and focused on the important part. "Cookies?" Dry or not, Mrs. Wixx's cookies were delicious.

"Of course," Mrs. Wixx said, pulling something big and round and wrapped in napkins out of her purse to hand to him and to Rhys who was standing quietly behind him. "I know how to tame big bad wolves."

"Ha, ha, very funny." Brayton plopped down across from her at the small table and took the cookie.

She handed him another napkin. "Make sure you eat over the napkins so you don't get crumbs everywhere. I don't want to get Ms. Carrier mad at me. The library might take offense." She finished with a huge wink.

"Rachel!" the librarian warned.

Was the wink code for something? He was never quite sure with Mrs. Wixx. Wait, was Mrs. Wixx serious about offending the library?

"I assume you're talking about the magical library," Brayton said.

"How do you know about the magical library? Did Honey tell you?" Ms. Carrier snapped.

Brayton would have rolled his eyes, but the new one Mrs. Wixx had given him felt weird when he did that. "Honey tell me something? Ha! No, it's just logic. There are witches in the school but no magic section in the library, so there must be a magical library somewhere. Not to mention, you reek of magic but it doesn't smell that way anywhere wolves can go."

"I reek?" the librarian said.

"To normal wolves. Honey wouldn't agree."

"Well that's comforting."

Ms. Carrier was a master of sarcasm.

"Does the library have a mind of its own," Brayton asked curiously.

"Not usually," Mrs. Wixx said, "but when my mother fired Ms. Carrier because, well because of an incident that brought unwanted attention, and tried to hire a person to take her place, the library shut all its doors and refused to open them until Ms. Carrier was hired again. My mother suspected Ms. Carrier had somehow spelled it to act that way but turns out it wasn't her."

"Who was it?" Brayton asked.

"Whoever caused the incident didn't want Ms. Carrier to get into trouble so they told the library to protect her."

Was this related to Honey's library break-in? He'd thought that was in Boston but worrying about getting people in trouble sounded like Honey. "That was nice."

"Except I was actually looking forward to traveling for a while," Ms. Carrier complained.

"And I think you should," Mrs. Wixx said. "We'll find someone to watch things for the summers so you can get out more. You shouldn't have to stay at the library all the time. Okay, Brayton let's see that eye."

"I'm going to check my mailbox," Ms. Carrier said hastily.

"There are things much grosser in the library," Mrs. Wixx chuckled when Ms. Carrier rushed out the door, "yet for some reason, your empty eye socket makes her squeamish. You're a regular librarian repellent."

"Thanks." He flipped up his eye patch and tried to roll his eyes again. "Rolling my eye feels weird."

"Do that often, do you?"

"More than I realized."

"Hmm, looks like you're a little tight on one side. I'm going to try and loosen it up. Sit still for a bit."

Mrs. Wixx put her fingers on his temple and a soothing smell that reminded him of lemon herbal tea flowed around them.

"Any news of my granddaughter?" Mrs. Wixx said conversationally.

He set his index finger and only his index finger on the table to indicate 'yes'. "I haven't heard anything."

"And how is your mother doing?"

He lifted his finger since that wasn't a yes or no question. "The same."

"Did you show her your eye?"

He put his middle finger down on the table even though he didn't need to since he could actually say 'no'. "No. I didn't want her to see it until it was finished."

"I understand. Try moving it now. Better?"

"Yes."

"Okay, move your eye patch to the other eye and we'll see if it works."

"What do you mean works?"

She gave him a sly smile. "I mean, let's see if you can see with it."

"Really?" He'd thought he was just getting a witch-made fake eye for looks.

"Really. You don't think I would give you just any old eye, do you? I'm a witch, for goodness sake. The color match is perfect, by the way."

"Good."

"Okay," she said once his other eye was covered, "Do you see anything at all?"

"Light?"

"Good. That means your optic nerve has started to adjust. It should get better and better over the next several weeks. Let's see if I can direct it a bit. Here, look down and tell me when you start to see shapes."

He heard a rustle of paper and then smelled lemon tea again. The white he was seeing all around turned brighter while a black shape started to form in the middle.

"Is it a black triangle?"

"Good. Is it clear?"

"Not really."

"Tell me when it's clear."

Mrs. Wixx's adjustments went on forever. Brayton's mind wandered. What was Honey doing? Had she written again? He itched to pull out the slate but it wasn't safe to do it in the librarian's office. Mrs. Wixx had made that clear their first meeting by shaking her head every time he tried to speak or write about Honey.

"There, that should do for now," she finally said. "Lift up your eye patch and see how they feel together."

He did as she asked and nearly threw up.

"Nauseous, huh," she said sympathetically when he quickly shut his eyes. "Believe it or not, you'll get used to it. You should continue wearing the eye patch though until your eye settles. "Oh, I almost forgot. Let's see if you can read letters." She pulled out another piece of paper. "What do you see?"

"It says 'Hi Brayton.'"

"Okay blink you eye and read it again. Is it still clear?"

He blinked. The words were still there but now they had a silver glow.

"Um, the words are.."

"Blurry?" she winked. "Hmm. Blink twice, very deliberately. Maybe the eye is just a bit loose."

It didn't feel loose. He blinked twice as instructed. Red letters appeared under the black ones that said 'Your new eye can see magic with one blink and hidden magic with two. Blink one more time to see normal again. No one else in the world has an eye like this. It was my great-uncle's."

"Um…" He wasn't quite sure what to say. He was wearing a dead witch's eye. On the other hand, it was magical and unique and he could see.

"Okay?" Mrs. Wixx asked. For the first time since he'd known her, she looked unsure.

She'd given him, a wolf, the ability to see magic, hidden magic that even wolf noses couldn't sniff out. He covered her smaller hand with his own. "Yes, thank you."

There was a glowing bug on the desk next to them. He blinked and it disappeared. He blinked twice and it came back. They'd been right to be cautious. Somebody was spying on them. He nonchalantly slammed his hand down over the bug, and looked around, searching for more suspicious objects. "Where did I put my keys? Did you notice if I had them in my hand when I came in?"

Mrs. Wixx looked from him to his hand, then back to him again. He nodded, then lifted up his hand. The bug was still there. Mrs. Wixx smirked at him and slid the ring off her thumb and handed it to him. "Can you read that?"

He looked down at the top of the ring. A strange symbol was etched into the top. "I see something, but I don't know what it says."

"Hmm. Tap what you see."

"What?"

She looked from him to the desk where he'd slammed his hand. "You should see a series of dots."

She was totally lying, but he got it. He touched the ring against the bug. It melted into a puddle of goo.

"That's all you see?"

He looked around, then at her. There was a super large glowing ladybug sitting on Mrs. Wixx's shoulder. He whacked it off with the ring.

"Yeah. Did you bring a mirror? I want to see how my eye looks."

"Of course. I know have vain you wolves are."

"Us! Have you seen the way the witches dress on this campus? And don't get me started on the hair!"

He looked at his shoulders without the mirror, then studied himself with it. There wasn't a bug, but something was glowing on his shoulder. He touched it with the ring. It disappeared in a puff of glowing smoke. Behind him, Rhys was pretending he wasn't paying attention, but Brayton knew he was observing and recording everything. Nothing glowed on Rhy's shoulders. The new eye, however, was glowing like a fireball in Brayton's head. He blinked and it looked completely normal.

"That's freaky," he mumbled.

"What is dear?"

"It looks completely normal, at least by itself." He flipped up his eye patch and immediately flipped it back down when his stomach protested. "And it will stay by itself for now."

"Tomorrow I want you to start using both eyes at once as long as you can stand it. After you can use them both without issue, we'll try a transformation. I know tonight is a full moon, but I want to be there the first time you transform with the eye installed."

"I remember." The eye had changed shape when he'd transformed with it before she started 'plugging it in' as she called it. It had felt fine then, but he hadn't realized then he'd be able to see as well as transform with it. She'd given him an amazing gift. He tapped his eye patch. "Thank you for this. I really, really appreciate it."

"It was the least I could do after what Gaian did." She shook her head. Grief dragged at her normally genial features and he was certain she was thinking of her daughter and the son-in-law she'd never met.

"This cookie is delicious, but it will taste even better with coffee," Brayton commented, holding up the half he had left. "There's a coffee place in the student union or we can go somewhere else." Hopefully that would be bug free or maybe they could go for a short walk on the grounds.

"The student union is fine. Don't forget to clean up after yourself," Mrs. Wixx said, nodding at the napkin.

"Yes, Mom."

"That's Grand-mom to you."

How weird would that be, to have her as a grand-mom? Not weird at all, he decided. He liked Mrs. Wixx. It was sad she hadn't even known she was a grand-mom until last year and now couldn't even get to know Honey.

He collected his cookie and his napkin and escorted Mrs. Wixx out of the library with Rhys following. By the way Mrs. Wixx babbled on about people he'd never heard of, he gathered she didn't think it was safe to talk outside even though there was no one close. They were almost to the student union. He had to find a way to talk to her before they were surrounded by people again.

"Mrs. Wixx, Honey…"

She cut him off. "You should try walking with your new eye and see if it refocuses properly as you move."

"But…"

"It's better you try while I'm here. I'm sorry I didn't think of it sooner. Go ahead. Look around. See if the sunlight bothers you at all."

"Okay."

He moved his eye patch over and opened his new eye, then quickly shut it. "Bright, it's too bright."

She pulled him off the path and under a large tree. "Really? It shouldn't be. Oh, I know, it's because you are a wolf. You're more sensitive to light. You can see better too, can't you. I need to adjust for that."

"You can do that? Wasn't this supposed to replace a witch's eye?"

"It's a magical eye and the maker added lots of features, including the ability to see in the dark, and when it is super bright."

"What about when I transform?"

"One problem at a time. Don't worry though, we'll get it to work. That's the nice thing about magic. If you want it bad enough, you can usually figure out how to do it."

She turned him so that his back was facing the sidewalk, probably so no one would see her, and put her fingers on his temples.

"Oh, yes, I see. There. How's that."

He risked a glance out onto the sunny lawn. "Better."

"Good. Blink a couple of times and look again. Still the same?"

"Yes. No?" A glowing body stood not five feet from where they were. He looked at Mrs. Wixx and raised an eyebrow. She wiggled hers back.

"What is it yes or no?"

"Yes," he said decisively while tapping his middle finger against his chest.

"Good. Let's go get that coffee."

He walked with his magic eye on the rest of the way to the student union and while he stood in line. He had the beginnings of a headache by the time they got their order and claimed their seats. He moved his eye patch over while Mrs. Wixx very deliberately took a coin out of her purse and set it in the middle of the table.

"You don't have to tip here."

"You can talk now. It's a special coin. It disrupts magical and mundane listening devices, prevents lipreading, and if anything crosses or is inside the barrier, it will warn us. I didn't want to use it in Lila's office because she would know what it was and I'm still not certain how trustworthy she is."

"You have a lot of interesting devices."

She chuckled. "Many of my Wixx ancestors were inventors or spell breakers like Honey. I'm an aberration. This coin was created by my great-great aunt during WWI. She was a spy."

"Wow. If your ancestors could break spells, does that mean they could also break curses? I thought Honey was unique in that."

"She is. Curses are spells laced with evil. You have to be able to both break the spell and defeat the evil. Now what did you want to tell me?"

Finally, he could talk. He hadn't even said anything to his friends in case his mom was somehow listening. "Honey's in trouble. She got hit on the head and I think she's lost at least part of her memory. She asked me where she was. I need a portal so I can go to her. I was hoping you might know how I could get one."

Mrs. Wixx took a slow sip of coffee. "She hit her head? Do you know how and when it happened?"

"She hasn't told me how it happened. She was fine on Friday. In fact, she found a clue about the curse, but when she wrote Saturday morning, our time, she sent a message asking *me* where she was. That's when I knew something was wrong, because she's never told me where she is."

"Sounds like I should be the one to go, not you. What kind of clue did she find?"

"There was a woman in a museum who had a vision about how the curse started. She knew the names of the originators, all except one, and why they started the curse."

"Why did they?"

"They thought relationships between witches and wolves were the cause of the Black plague. Can you go to her?"

Mrs. Wixx let out a long sigh. "I wish I could more than anything, but Mother and the rest of the witching world are watching me closely. I've no doubt the only reason Mother hasn't complained much about me helping you is because she thinks I'll lead her to Honey."

"What would your mother do if she found Honey?"

Mrs. Wixx studied her coffee cup. "Test her. Use her. Possibly turn her over to the witch council."

"Is there anyone else you'd trust to help her?"

"No, but I could make a healing charm. It may not bring back her memory, but it will heal anything that needs healing. If her memory is not permanently damaged, it will help." She took another contemplative sip of her coffee. "You don't have wards around your pack lands, right?"

"We're wolves," he scoffed.

"I try not to assume things. Someone would notice if I had anything delivered to our coven thanks to our wards. I'll order some portals and have them portal-shipped to you. The package should appear on your bed."

"Can they make it show up in my backpack or under the bathroom cabinet? Mom keeps searching my room."

"Mmm." She plopped her big purse on the table and started searching through it. After several moments, she pulled out a business card and handed it to him. "Put this where you want it to go."

The card was cream colored with a vine in black ink around the edge and Mrs. Wixx's name in fancy black letters in the middle, but nothing else, not even on the back.

"It's my business card," she said.

"Okay?"

"You can use it to contact me. You hold it and say who you are and what you need, but that's not why I gave it to you. I'll show one to the portal man and he'll be able to target wherever you put that one."

"Wow, thanks."

"As soon as you have the portals and you know where you can meet Honey, contact me and we can meet here. I'll take another look at your eye, then you can take the healing charm to her."

The sudden relief that he'd be able to finally do something hit him like a wave. He grabbed Mrs. Wixx's hand and squeezed. "Thank you."

Mrs. Wixx twisted her hand so that she could hold his back. "No, thank you, Brayton. I'm glad she has such a good friend."

He looked down, in part to hide the moisture gathering in his eye. "I wasn't always."

"But you are now though, and that's what's important."

"I guess," not that it had done her much good.

"Oh, right," she touched the ring now on Brayton's pinky, "that was also Uncle's, but you may not need it. With practice, you should be able to shoot the equivalent of a magical laser at spells and destroy them that way, assuming it will work the same way with a wolf as it did with a witch."

He blinked, then wondered if it was safe to close his eye. "My new eye shoots laser beams?"

"More like laser blasts I think, and I don't believe anyone other than you will be able to see them and they'll only work on spells."

"How do I make it blast things?"

She rubbed her chin thoughtfully. "Think about what you want and give it to yourself. If you practice in a mirror, make sure you are looking at an angle so you don't shoot yourself in the eye. That eye is the only one of those I have."

"Right. Don't shoot myself in my magical eye with my anti-magic laser beams." He glanced at Rhys. His normally impassive friend's eyebrows were so high, Brayton bust out laughing.

Mrs. Wixx patted him on the shoulder. "That's the spirit."

13

BRAYTON – AUGUST 19 – INDIANA

"So…" Rhys began.

"Not now," Brayton said quickly, looking around the campus parking garage with his magical eye. He didn't see anyone or anything glowing around them, but that didn't mean someone wasn't spying on them.

Rhys unlocked his truck. Brayton opened the passenger door and stared in shock.

"What's wrong?" Rhys asked, sliding into the driver's seat right on top of two of the little glowing insects that were fluttering around the cab.

"Nothing." Brayton swiped the ring over the three in his seat, turning them to magical goo. Nasty. He reluctantly slid into the seat. He couldn't see a thing with his normal sight, but he was changing his pants when he got home.

"So…" Rhys tried again after Brayton had slammed the door.

"Not now."

Where had all the bugs come from? Had witches broken into Rhys' truck while they were talking to Mrs. Wixx or had they been there before? Good thing Honey was so secretive or he might have told his friends where she was without realizing they were being spied on. As it was, his friends knew about the slate but he hadn't told them where he'd hidden it. He swiped his hand with the ring at the line of bugs watching him from the dash. Most of them were shaped like grasshoppers or long-legged crickets but were all bigger than any grasshoppers he'd ever seen. The ring instantly melted them. He tried to laser blast the ones behind the steering wheel, but that only made his headache worse. Leaning over to swipe at the ones around his feet made him feel nauseous. He finally gave up and laid his head back on the seat.

"You okay?" Rhys asked.

"Yeah, just a bit of a headache."

"So the eye was…"

"Shh. It's not safe."

"We are moving on a road. There's no one else here."

"Have you checked your cab for bugs lately?"

"Seriously? You are starting to act as paranoid as that old woman."

"She has good reason to be paranoid. She knows what magic can do. Let's not talk for now. I'm tired. Can you put on some music?"

"Sure." The worry in Rhys' voice made him feel guilty, but who knew who those bugs were reporting to and how many were hiding under the seats.

His mom ambushed him the instant he stepped in the door. "How did it go?"

"Fine, mom."

"You should have told me when you were leaving. I wanted to go. I have questions."

"I'm sure Mrs. Wixx wouldn't mind if you called her. I have her number."

"Can I see it? Is it all fixed now?"

"Sure." He switched his eye patch to his other eye and opened his new one.

"It looks good. Let me see them together."

"Not yet mom. I have to get used to using them separately first. It's still adjusting."

"You can see with it?"

"Yep. As Mrs. Wixx said, she is a witch. She wouldn't just give me a glass eye. It even adjusts to the light and moves just like a real one."

"Well why couldn't she have magicked a real eye back into your head?" his mom huffed.

"I guess even witches have limits."

He blinked once and looked around. Nothing magical except the calendar Mom had bought at the witches' craft sale last year that always had the correct day circled. He blinked twice. Whoa. There were bugs everywhere and his mom had something stuck to the side of her head that looked like an antenna. He pulled her into a hug, then brushed his left pinky, which was the only finger the ring would fit on, against the spell on her head like he was fixing her hair. "I love you Mom."

"Oh, Brayton," she squeezed him tightly. "I love you too. You're not still mad at me for making you stay home from college are you?"

"No, Mom." He looked down. There was a spell on her back too. He vanished it with a touch, then released her. "I'm going to take a shower. Being around witches makes me feel…" he shivered.

"I know what you mean."

His room was full of bugs. There was even one attached to his phone. The bathroom wasn't much better. Did that mean whoever it was knew about the slate? If so, why hadn't his mom found it? Maybe they didn't realize what it was. He turned all the creatures into goo, including the three in the sink cabinet, stripped, checked himself for more spells in the mirror, then pulled out the slate.

His last message was still there. He turned on the water so it would get hot and wrote:

Dear Wasp.

[Aug. 19, 4:30 pm]. I'm coming with a healing spell. Tell me where to meet you and what time. If I miss the time, I'll come anyway. I'll be checking my slate as often as I can. Stay safe.

He tucked it away and stepped into the shower.

An hour later, he was ready for another shower. He knew they were just spells, but every time he tapped the ring against one of the many magic bugs he'd found hidden all through the house they melted or splattered. It was gross. How long would it take whoever had placed all the spells to figure out he was destroying them and place more?

"Brayton, what are you doing up there?" Mom asked behind him.

"I was looking for something."

"What? No one has touched those books in years."

"I know. I found a lot of dust." He sneezed to emphasize the point.

"Maybe I should put you to good use then. Stay there. I'll get the duster."

Phooey. She was probably going to make him clean house until she decided it was time for the pack run. He shouldn't have mentioned the dust. He still had half the house to debug.

"I have to find this first, Mom. I can help you dust later," he called after her. If there was a later. How long would it take Mrs. Wixx to make the charm? Had the portals come yet? He was tempted to check the empty shoe box where he'd put Mrs. Wixx's card in his closet, but he couldn't do anything until Honey responded.

His dad's office was oddly clean of bugs, although there were plenty in the hallway right outside. Did the office have a protective spell he didn't know about? He couldn't see a spell around the door. He closed his magic eye to give his brain a rest and waved his hand around in the general vicinity of the bugs, only opening his eye again when he hit the wall. His head and his stomach both protested while the new eye focused again. He wouldn't be able to keep this up much longer, but he wanted to get rid of the bugs before he left.

"Brayton, what are you doing?" Dad asked behind him.

He turned to look at his dad with his finger over his lips and quickly regretted moving so fast. Flipping his eye patch over so he could see with his good eye, he opened the door to his father's office, dragged him inside, and shut the door firmly behind them.

"Brayton?"

Brayton tapped his lips with his finger again and did a full walk around his father with his eye patch up to make sure he was clean before he took his finger down and spoke.

"There are magical bugs coating the wall outside your office. I was destroying them."

"Excuse me?"

Brayton tapped the cheek under his new eye. "Magical eye can see hidden magic. Mrs. Wixx also gave me a ring to destroy spells. Our house is infested. I didn't find any in here though."

Dad went to his desk and sat down. "Maybe because of this." He pulled a paper weight shaped like a golf ball out of his top drawer and placed it on the desk. With Brayton's magical sight, it glowed a bright white. He'd always wondered why his dad had a golf ball paperweight when he didn't play golf.

"Where did you get that?"

"Your mom's mother gave it to us for a wedding present. She said it would keep the witches away."

"Does it work?"

"Well until now, I haven't had a chance to test it. Have you checked your mother's office yet?"

"No."

"Let's take a look."

Brayton opened the door to his mother's office, peered in, and wished he hadn't. Magical bugs were everywhere. Some looked like they were reproducing. There was no way he could exterminate them all tonight. He shut the door and backed away.

"That bad?" Dad asked.

Brayton nodded and swiped at one that had flown out and landed on his father's shoulder. Dad pointed toward his office. This time he was the one to shut the door.

"They're swarming in Mom's office. It would take me all night to get rid of all of them."

"One of the witches at the college must have bugged her. How bad is the rest of the house?"

"My room was pretty bad. There were about twenty in the living room that I found. I haven't checked your bedroom yet. Mom had an antenna sticking off her head. It was the first thing I destroyed."

"Are you sure you're seeing what you think you're seeing? I mean, Mrs. Wixx seems nice, but why would she give you an eye that can see magic?"

"It was her great-uncle's eye. Yeah, kind of gross if you think about it," Brayton admitted when his dad flinched. "I'm trying not to. I think she gave it to me so I can help protect Honey. I can see normal things with it too."

"What happens if you transform with it?"

"It should transform with me, but Mrs. Wixx told me not to transform tonight. She wants to be there the first time I try, and she wants it to be fully functional with my human form first."

"Makes sense I suppose. As to the bugs, kill as many as you can. I'll tell your mom we found some bugs inside her office and to keep the door shut so they don't spread. I'll also call around and see if I can find a magical exterminator."

"I could ask Mrs. Wixx."

"I'd rather get a second opinion to make sure that eye is working correctly."

"Sure."

"And Brayton,"

"Yes, Dad."

"I'm proud of you."

14

HONEY – AUGUST 24 – UNITED KINGDOM

Honey groaned and made herself stand. She couldn't wait any longer. She needed water and maybe some food. Why was it so hard to walk straight? Stupid girl and her stupid poison. Who carries around a syringe full of poison or even owns one? She coughed up and expelled another glob of phlegm. Ugh her chest hurt. Was Annia experiencing any of this or had she lied about the antidote? It hadn't smelled like a lie, but after four days of being as sick as she'd ever been in her life, Honey wouldn't be upset to learn the antidote wasn't 100% effective.

She crawled out from under the trees she'd taken refuge under the day after her arrival and stood for a moment enjoying the warmth of the sun on her fur. For the first time since departing Rome, she almost felt warm. The UK was surprisingly cool in the summer, and more rural than she expected.

Had this area been more populated when they built Stonehenge or had the builders chose this spot because it wasn't populated? Were the roads that existed now anywhere close to the roads that had existed back then?

She started walking east still in wolf form across the field, far enough from the highway that the passing cars couldn't easily see her. Had people once trekked across the same field to get to the stones? Maybe they'd lived in the town she was pretty sure was ahead, at least she hoped there was a town ahead. If not, she was going to have to come up with another plan.

Ten minutes later, she came upon a road that branched off from the main one called Stonehenge Road. Even more promising, she could see buildings lining it in the not-so-distant distance and there was a narrow, paved walking trail right beside the road. Buildings and trails meant food. She transformed behind a tree and pulled a hoodie from her backpack, then leaned against the tree while she recovered from pulling it over her head. This was ridiculous. She'd never been so sick. Was this what the flu felt like or was it worse?

The road kept going and going, at first past more fields, than past some old-looking thatched houses, but not one of them was a restaurant or a store. Did these people not eat? Where did they buy their groceries? She kept trudging along and finally the houses started getting closer to the road and closer together. Businesses became common. The first restaurant looked to be closed. The second was more promising, considering it was open, but something that smelled even better wasn't far ahead. Until that moment she hadn't really felt hungry, but the beefy, cheesy fragrance of the pizza and hamburger take-out place was like a trumpet blast to her sleeping stomach and her dormant salivary glands.

Ten minutes later she was sitting in the sunshine at one of the outdoor tables, stuffing her mouth with the first hot food she'd had in days, and washing it down with a huge bottle of water. She already felt better – much, much better. She finished off her last fry, then leaned back and wiped her mouth while furtively looking around to see if anyone was paying attention. No one was. She pulled out her magic slates. Someone had written "Hi sunshine" on the guys' slate. She was pretty sure that was Nathan. She sent back a smiley face. Brayton's slate, on the other hand, was covered. He'd written four more times since she'd last wrote to him right after she'd portalled to the UK.

Dear Wasp [Aug 20, 11:12pm] I'm glad you got away and that you remember everything. I keep finding little magical spies everywhere. I swear I kill one and the next day there are two. The magical exterminator, who was a wolf, by the way, said he'd never seen such a bad infestation. That's what he called it. Is it truly an infestation if they are spells and not insects?

Dear Wasp[Aug 21, 10:02pm] Not much happened here today. Did you find what you were looking for?

Dear Wasp[Aug 22, 5:12pm] Did something happen? Why aren't you writing?

Aug 23, 8am. Please tell me you're okay.

Honey lifted the sheet, erasing his words and wrote:

Dear BB [daytime]. I'm okay. Sorry for not writing. I got sick. It was awful. I'm better now. I found some food. Do you know if there are other people that can shift into animals? Remember how the

147

Egyptians worshiped gods that were part human and part animal? Do you think they were shifters? If so, what happened to them? Why are there only wolves now? I will start searching for the place I saw in the vision tomorrow.

To her surprise, her words disappeared almost immediately and were replaced by Brayton's remarkably neat handwriting.

OMG, I was so worried. If you tell me where you are, I can bring you a healing charm. Your Gma made one when I told her about your head.

I'm okay. I'm feeling better since I ate. Do people still say OMG?

Are you sure? Is getting sick normal for you? And yes, they do.

Yes, no, and I know old women use it, but I don't think it was ever in style for our age group, just saying.

How would you know? You don't have a phone and when you did, you never had it on!

Not true. You just always tried to call me when it was off. Your bad timing was not my fault. Doesn't school start next week? I miss beating you in practice.

How can you miss beating me if it never happened? Are you sure you got your memory back? It's not going to be the same without you. I wish you were here.

Me too.

15

BRAYTON – SEPTEMBER 10 – INDIANA

WOLF class wasn't the same without Honey. Nothing was, although most of that had nothing to do with her. Online classes were boring. He switched back to in-person classes on the days he had to drive to school anyway, then started crashing on the couch in his friends' dorm. Mom, surprisingly, didn't complain all that much. The worst part was not having a meal plan, but if Honey could buy groceries and survive out in a tent by herself then he could certainly get his rear to the store and survive on a couch.

He spent a lot of time in the library, probably more in the first week than in an entire semester last year. It made it easy to meet up with Mrs. Wixx who, after three weeks of adjustments, finally gave him the go-ahead to try a transformation in the librarian's office. From the way her lip curled and one nostril lifted, Brayton could tell the librarian was less than pleased about the situation, but at least she didn't stay to watch. Mrs. Wixx, on the other hand, was so straightforward about everything, except for the fact that she was Honey's grandmother, it didn't bother him to stand naked in front of her. It helped that she was completely focused on his face and Rhys was there.

"Stop if you feel anything pulling or if anything feels uncomfortable."

"Okay."

She stepped back and gave a nod and a warm smile. "Go ahead."

He'd never thought too much about how all his body parts had to change when he transformed, but now it seemed like he could feel everything except, oddly, the eye.

"How is it? Can you see?"

Brayton closed his good eye and looked around, then nodded.

"Does it look right?"

He shook his head.

"He says it's not quite focused and he sees in color," Rhys spoke for him.

"Is that a problem, the color thing," Mrs. Wixx asked, putting her hands on Brayton's head.

"No, just different," Rhys said.

"Then I won't worry about it. I'm not really sure how to fix it and I might end up making you see in black and white all the time, or worse, in reverse, like a negative." She tilted Brayton's head to the side so she could see his eye better, than ran her hand down the middle of his head. "Wow, your fur is really soft."

"He says thanks," Rhys supplied.

She put her hand back on the top of his head and sighed. "You know, I don't even know what Honey's fur feels like. It looked soft when I saw her. She was a lot smaller than you though."

Brayton nodded. He didn't know what her fur felt like either. Sure they'd run together a few times, but he'd never touched her when he was human, not like Mrs. Wixx was patting him now. The hollow, achy feeling in his chest gave a painful pulse.

"I'm worried about her, out there all alone. It's not good for a girl her age, or anyone really, to be all alone."

He blinked once. Everything that was magical was glowing as it should. He blinked again and searched the room. He'd done it once already as a human and hadn't seen anything, but better to be safe.

There, at the top of the bookshelf, the little critter probably thought he wouldn't spot his magical antenna. The critter was wrong. Unfortunately, he couldn't easily reach the top of the shelf in this form and Rhys wouldn't be able to see if there were more than one.

"Have you heard anything from her? Anything at all?"

The timing of the question was so out of character for Mrs. Wixx, that he automatically focused on her face to see what message she was really trying to convey. The sudden change in focus made his stomach roll unpleasantly, but only until the focus of his new eye caught up with his old one. Oddly, she looked sincere, like she was actually expecting him to answer in the librarian's bugged office.

"He says the eye isn't refocusing properly. There's a delay," Rhys said for him.

"Answer the question," Mrs. Wixx snapped.

That was not Mrs. Wixx, or at least she wasn't in full control. He blinked twice to reset the eye to see normal magic. Mrs. Wixx was glowing faintly, like she usually did when she was working on his eye, but at the moment she wasn't doing magic. Was someone using magic on her? He warned Rhys then started to transform back.

"What are you doing? We need to test a few more things."

"He can transform back again," Rhys said. "He wanted to see if the eye still worked the same when he transformed back."

Mrs. Wixx nodded and stepped back to give him room, although he didn't need it. He finished the transformation and grabbed his shorts.

"Aren't you going to transform back?" Mrs. Wixx asked when he started to pull them on.

"In a moment."

He put his hand in his pocket and pushed his pinky into the ring, then pulled a chair over to the bookcase. Whatever the creature was supposed to be, it was ugly. The size of two cats stuck end-to-end, it had the body of a lizard, teeth jutting out in random positions from a wide mouth, and one antenna that wiggled about in front of everything. The only good thing about it was instead of exploding, it melted when he tapped it with the ring. After taking a careful look at all the other shelves he couldn't see properly from the floor, he climbed back down and put the chair back in the exact spot he'd found it. He suspected the librarian would probably refuse to let them come back if anything was even a hair out of place.

Mrs. Wixx was no longer glowing, but that could just mean whoever it was wasn't exerting their power just now. Should he tap her with the ring? She'd held it, shoot, he wore it, and he was still fine, so it likely wouldn't hurt her, but it probably had to have direct contact with the spell to destroy it. Should he just reschedule? No. He couldn't leave her like this. What if whoever was in her head made her do something she'd regret? He walked over to the desk and picked up the little bell the librarian had left and gave it a firm shake.

"What's wrong Brayton? Why did you ring for the librarian?"

Mrs. Wixx looked honestly confused.

He didn't get a chance to answer before the librarian came charging in through a backdoor Brayton hadn't realized was there.

"What it is Rachel, what did they do?"

"WE didn't do anything," Brayton informed her. "I think someone spelled her and took control of her mind for a moment. She was asking me things and demanding things she never would normally. I was hoping you'd have a way to check and make sure she's okay."

"What are you talking about, Brayton?" Mrs. Wixx asked.

"You don't remember asking me about Honey?"

"I didn't ask you about Honey."

The librarian frowned and walked over to a filing cabinet in the corner. After retrieving a stick about two feet long from beside it, she turned to Mrs. Wixx and started waving it around.

"What are you doing?" Mrs. Wixx demanded.

"Just checking."

The stick whined, especially when the librarian waved it over Mrs. Wixx's stomach.

"She's carrying a spell, likely ingested," Ms. Carrier proclaimed, moving the stick away then back toward Mrs. Wixx's stomach several times.

"I haven't…" Mrs. Wixx stamped her foot. "ooo…I knew there was something fishy going on when Mom invited Mrs. Nevermore over. She doesn't even like the woman. I hope you're listening, you old hags!"

"Can they hear you from your stomach?" Brayton asked curiously. Did she have one of those magical bugs inside her and if so, how had it gotten in?

"Maybe, but it would have to be a very strong spell to take over completely as it seems to have done, then relay whatever was said. It's easier to just attach a listening device somewhere on the target," the librarian replied, still scanning. "It might not even be magical."

"Knowing my mother, it's magical." Mrs. Wixx let out a long sigh. "We're going to have to call it a day. I don't want to try and adjust anything with those two in my head. At least we know you can transform with it and it's functional enough for now."

"How did they get a spell inside you? Did they spell your food or something?" Brayton asked. Should he be checking his food at all times with his magical eye?

"They probably switched out my vitamin for the spell. I knew I should have had more than one left yesterday."

"How will you get rid of it?" he asked.

Mrs. Wixx raised an eyebrow at him. "How do you normally get rid of things you eat that you can't digest?"

"Oh."

"Let's plan to meet again on Friday after your classes. Sound good?"

"Sure."

Mrs. Wixx reached up and patted him on the shoulder. "Don't sound so dejected. It's only a couple of days and you should be in full working order by the full moon."

"I know. I was more concerned about you."

She touched his cheek and smiled, but her eyes shimmered with tears. "You are such a sweet boy, even if you are a wolf. Don't worry about me. Mom means well, she always has."

Darn it. He pulled her into a hug and closed his eyes to keep the tears in his own under control when he thought of how difficult it was to be around his own mom anymore. "Yeah, moms usually do."

16

HONEY – OCTOBER 17 – SCOTLAND

Honey walked a full circle to look and sniff around on top of the half-buried tunnels she'd found not too far off the coast she'd been following for weeks. No scents other than that of wet plant life, rodents, and a faint whiff of salty air assuaged her nostrils and the only things standing were trees. The place was quite eerie, actually, with the abandoned equipment and train tracks that must have been important to someone at some time but were now overgrown with weeds and trees. At least she'd have a roof over her head in case it started raining again and maybe her tent would finally get a chance to dry out. She let gravity pull her down the steep slope beside one of the tunnel entrances. If she could find some dry grass she could use it to insulate the wet ground between the tracks. Even better, she could start a fire and be warm for a while. Nobody would see it down in the middle of the sunken pit if she kept it small.

An hour later, she pulled her already upright tent from the nether so that it landed perfectly on the square of grass she'd collected. The grass wasn't quite dry, but that's what tarps and sleeping bags were for. Next came her backpack and the ten delicious-smelling tacos she'd picked up that made her both salivate and feel sad. She plopped down on the cut log she'd acquired somewhere in Wales and pulled out her magic slates. The guys were probably still in class and it was…Wednesday or Thursday. Hmm. It wasn't like it mattered.

Her last message was still on the guys' slate, whoever had it today, probably Luca, hadn't woken up in time to read it.

[19:00] I've got tacos! What did you guys have? Ran past a ridiculous number of golf courses today. That is a sport I do not understand. Hugs.

Maybe she shouldn't have mentioned tacos and golf, or maybe it would make people think she was in Mexico. Did they play golf in Mexico? She shrugged and dug into her tacos. Who knew running twenty miles a day would give her the magical ability to make tacos disappear as fast as the guys?

She wiped the last of the taco juice from her face and hands before finally pulling out Brayton's slate. He had written in the morning and again after class.

[October 17, 6am]. Hi Beautiful. Have a lovely day.

[1:00 pm]. OH MY GOSH. That test was HARD! My brain hurts. Kidding. I think I did good. Anything exciting happen today?

She erased his words and wrote:

158

[October 17, 19:10]. If by exciting, you mean nearly getting nailed with a couple of golf balls, then yes. No luck finding what I need though. I'm not really expecting it here, but there are some promising sites close. I just need to find a way to get there.

She waited to see if he would respond but no new letters appeared. She blinked away a tear. When was the last time she'd talked to someone, truly talked, not just wrote?

Wait. That would be today, when she ordered her tacos. Ha! And, they hadn't looked at her funny when she tried speaking with a British accent. Double Ha. She scribbled another line.

Also, I think I've mastered the local dialect, enough to order food anyway.

After staring at the unresponsive slate for several more minutes, she sighed and tucked it away. "Guess I'll go to bed since I forgot to buy more marshmallows."

Like she did every night, she pulled out the book of maps she'd acquired in a used bookstore and drew a line through the towns she'd passed and marked any stones she'd found. Most sites were already known, but there were a few places where she'd smelled old magic which might have once had stones that didn't have any current-day signs or markers. None of them had smelled cursed or evil though. She also marked where she'd smelled wolves, which was mostly in the sparsely populated areas between towns. She hadn't smelled any wolves where she was currently camped but she decided to sleep as a human just in case. If anyone noticed her, she could always tell them she was 'wild camping', which was a thing apparently, especially in Scotland.

Somewhere, at least a mile away, wolves howled. Funny how humans insisted there were no wolves roaming free in Scotland. Did they truly believe those were dogs? She went to the bathroom (aka bush), brushed her teeth, said her prayers, and climbed into the puffy pink sleeping bag she'd found at a yard sale.

Her intruder alarm didn't work.

It was only after someone kicked her foot that she heard the bells go off along with several undecipherable cuss words and the stuttering steps of someone tripping over the string.

"Yoo. Up."

She rubbed her eyes to give herself time to assess the situation. A wolf with a Scottish accent stood at the mouth of her tent and he'd been out running based on his nakedness. He hadn't attacked her yet, so that was promising.

"Yoo're trespassing in our territory."

"Sorry," she said with as low a voice as she could in her newly acquired British accent.

"Why arenae ye runnin' wi' th' moon?"

"Pardon?"

"Yoo're th' wolf who's been runnin' up th' coest th' lest month, arenae ye?"

Phooey. She should have known the wolf packs would notice and warn each other. There went her human cover. She sent her grandmother's charm to the nether in case she had to let her air shield fall.

"Yoo're a hen."

"I'm a what?"

Another shadowy figure appeared at the front of her tent. "Woman, eejit. Ye cannae go aroond callin' chicks hens."

Fudge and double-fudge. Stupid wolf noses. They could probably smell her scent from the few times she'd let her shield down in the tent, or maybe it was the pink sleeping bag, or maybe it was her hair. She should have had it cut at the barber earlier today. "I'm just passing through. I'll leave in the morning."

"Nae. Come run wi' us, then we will drink."

"I'm tired. I ran almost all day."

"It wisnae a request."

Was it her imagination or was he puffing up a bit? Great, an alpha.

"Fine, but I'm not getting naked in front of you. Please wait outside."

As soon as he stepped back, Honey zipped herself inside. She hated to leave her tent here, but if she made it disappear, they'd know who she was…or would they? She retrieved her backpack from the nether and dug around until she found the charmed ring she'd used to break into the museum. Since she didn't have a chain, she looped her hairband/anti-spying charm onto the ring then slipped the band back on her wrist. After sending her backpack back to the nether, she transformed, consciously retaining only the band. All the rest of her clothes were replaced by her thick reddish fur and the doggy backpack she'd found discarded or perhaps purposely lost by some pampered pooch on one of the many beaches she'd passed.

At least a dozen wolves, all bigger and fluffier than her, were waiting when she stepped out of the tent. The largest, who smelled like the first man, sniffed at her head.

She felt naked without her air shield, but he'd notice if she didn't smell like a wolf or didn't have a pack mark. She must still be pack, because he nodded and turned to lead his people out of the hole she was camping in. Honey tapped her wrist twice against the tent, then followed him, pretending that she didn't notice the surprised looks from the other wolves.

They didn't go far. In less than a mile, she was in the midst of a tidy trailer park surrounded by fields on all sides. A decent-sized bonfire was already burning in the center of the park with women and children tending it. All the wolves around her started to transform. Honey sat down and waited. A pretty woman with a baby on her hip handed the alpha some clothes and gave him a kiss. He pulled them on, accepted a beer from another guy, then finally turned his attention onto her.

"Yoo're a stubborn one, arenae ye? Come en."

He led her through the crowd, exchanging words, most of them not quite English, and back slaps with nearly everyone they passed. The people looked at her curiously, but didn't try to slap her, for which she was grateful. The man pulled open the door to a white trailer and gestured inside. "Ye can transform in haer. Nae a body will bortha ye as long as ye dornt take tay long."

The place smelled like baby and him and what must be the woman. She transformed the moment he shut the door but made herself count slowly to 120 before she emerged, adjusting her beanie like she'd just pulled it on. Her host pushed off the wall where he was leaning when she stepped out.

"Now aye ken you didnae hav' all those clothes in tha' wee pack."

"No. That's for food," she admitted, and to make humans think she had an owner somewhere, but she didn't say that. "I have a charm that allows me to stash what I need in the nether." She lifted her wrist to show him. "It's a lot easier than carrying everything."

"Yoo're yoong."

She nodded.

"Why are ye travelin' by yerself?"

"Gap year."

Usually that was enough to stop the questions, but instead of nodding sagely, he frowned at her. Could he tell it was a lie? It wasn't, not really. She just hoped it was only a year.

"Why isnae anyone from yer pack wi' ye?"

She shrugged as nonchalantly as she could. "I've always been a loner." But not completely alone, not until recently. She dropped into a squat and pretended she'd forgotten to tie her shoe. Stupid tears. Now wasn't the time.

To Honey's surprise, he threw his arm around her shoulders when she stood. "Isnae good tae be alone. Come meet mah Fiona."

Fiona turned out to be his wife, not his daughter. His daughter was about nine months old and could stuff her entire fist in her mouth.

"Haer sit." Her host pushed her towards the end of the wooden bench where his wife was seated. "Noo tell us about yerself."

"Um…" What could she say that wouldn't clue them in to who she was? Had they even heard about the hybrid the whole US was looking for?

His wife whacked his chest with the back of her hand. "Ye cannae just put folks on th' spot like 'at. At least introduce yerself first."

He gave his wife a squinty-eyed look, then thrust his hand toward Honey. "Mac."

Honey gripped his callused, beefy hand and shook it firmly. "Nice to meet you, Mac."

"An' yer name?" he hinted after several long moments of shaking.

What to tell him? She had so many aliases she was scared to give him one lest she forget. "Guess."

"Guess?" His eyes shot to his wife as if he'd never heard the word.

Why couldn't that be her name? "You know, like guest, but without the 'T'."

"That's a…er unique name," he said slowly.

"Thank you."

Honey took a sip of the beer someone had put in front of her. As beer went, it wasn't bad, still bitter though.

"Why don't ye tell us a bit about yer trip?" Fiona suggested after a long, quiet minute. "Seen anythin' interesting?"

"Lots of things." Everyone around the table went quiet like they were expecting her to say more. Should she? Maybe they'd know of some places she should go.

"What kinds of things?" Fiona prompted.

"Oh, you know, water, waves, sea birds, sand. Ocean stuff. I saw a lot of golf courses today."

"I'll bet. Were ye in wolf form?"

"Aye." Ha, she was already picking up the accent, or maybe that was Canadian. "They kept trying to hit me with the balls but I was too fast."

"Waste ay perfectly good land," Mac mumbled under his breath.

"Where are ye headed?" Fiona tried again.

"All the way around the UK."

"Why?" the guy standing next to Mac asked.

Honey recognized his voice. He was the one who had cursed her intruder alarm. She liked the way these wolves blurted out their thoughts. She wished she could. It would sure be a lot easier if she didn't have to lie.

Maybe she didn't.

"I'm looking for magic."

They all blinked at her like she'd said she was looking for UFOs and little green men.

"Haven't you noticed that all the standing stones and stone rings around the UK smell faintly of magic?" she continued, "Old magic, I mean."

"Naaee, can't say that ah've sniffed the stones or wanted tae," Mac said slowly. "Why would there be magic?"

"They were built back when people believed in magic and we know magic existed back then, in fact, it's likely that magic was used to build some of the rings. Plus, over the years, people would have performed a lot of spells at the sites. Most of the sites I've been to, the real sites, not the imagined ones, smell faintly of magic. I'm looking for lost sites, basically places that still smell of old magic but the posts or stones are gone. I imagine there were a lot of places of worship, perhaps one in every village, kind of like churches are now. There was probably a network of roads along the coast so people could travel and trade at the different villages."

"Why dae ye care?" Mac asked. "Tha' was a lang time ago."

She shrugged. "I like history."

"Seems like a waste ay time tae me."

His wife whacked Mac's chest again. "Leave 'er alone. Jist cause ye hae responsibilities now doesnae mean yae have tae be nasty tae folks 'at don't."

"I'm making a map. I might write a book someday," Honey chimed in. "Or a thesis paper. You guys know of any sites around here…within view of the water?"

"Why th' water?" Mac asked.

"I had to limit myself somehow, else I'll be running around the UK the rest of my life."

"Ur nae a complete eejit then."

"Mac!" his wife scolded.

"Can ye really smell magic aroond th' stones?" the other man asked.

"Aye, especially when I'm in wolf form."

"I'm Jay," the man said, thrusting his hand at her, "Mac's handsomer, smarter cousin. Ah ken a place. I'll take ye thaur tomorrow."

"Thank you."

17

HONEY – NOVEMBER 6 – SCOTLAND

"Guess."

Honey pulled herself out of her thoughts with a shake of her head. "Hmm?"

"I've bin callin' yer name for th' lest minute. What are ye thinkin' about sae hard?" Jay asked.

She tapped the map on her legs. "Planning. There's a ferry to the bigger island but what about the little ones around it? Maybe we should charter a boat."

"Ah highly doobt thaur are any stones worth mentionin' on any of those islands, an' definitely nae magic worth mentionin'. Witches don't like water."

"Says who?"

"Everybody."

She rolled her eyes. "Stop trying to gaslight me. I know you don't believe that."

"Nae, it's true."

She wished it were true. There were so many little islands around the big islands in the Hebrides, it was going to take months to do a thorough search. Maybe she could buy a boat and sell it when she was done.

"Ay doobt anyone would hae put a ring on an island anyway," Jay continued. "It would hae bin tae hard for folks tae visit."

"That's true," she conceded, drawn again to the map. There was something about this area, although she'd be hard-pressed to explain what. Maybe her parents were guiding her or maybe this was how curse-breakers felt around a strong curse. She could only hope.

"Guess."

"Yeah."

"Look at me."

She lifted her head and peered into Jay's amber eyes over the flames of their small fire. Despite how untrimmed his beard was, he was handsome, in an older guy kind of way.

"Why, is something wrong with you, something more I mean," she snarked.

"Funay. Nae, ay need tae tell you somethin'"

"What?"

"Ay have tae go home."

"Oh." She'd wondered how long he was going to hang around. She was still surprised he'd followed her a month ago. "I'm sorry to hear that. I've enjoyed traveling with you and I will miss your company, but I understand. You only planned to go away for a night and you have a job to get back to."

He gave her a stern look. "Ye should go home tay."

She smiled and gave him the best non-committal answer she could think of. "I will eventually."

"Nae eventually," he said sternly, "Now. It's nae safe fur ye tae be on yer own. Thaur are men an' wolves who

168

would tak' advantage ay a lassie like ye. They'll sneak up on ye when yoo're sleepin' an'…"

"Like you did?" she interrupted.

"Aye, but they'll be on ye before yer bells stop ringin'."

"And before they stop cussing," she teased.

"Ah am serious!"

"I know." She glanced down at the map again. It made sense for him to go now. This was the last large island close to his pack before she headed north. "How soon will you go?"

"Tomorrow."

"After we go to the island? It will only take half-a-day and you said you've never been."

"So, ye *can* listen."

"Always, but if you don't want to go, that's okay too. I'm sure that girl who works in the coffee shop will be glad to see you again and you can tell her all about the weird girl who sniffs stones."

"Tha' woold be the shortest conversation ever," he grumbled. "I've bin travelin' wi' ye for weeks an' that's still all ah know about ye. Ye huvnae e'en told me yer real name."

"How do you know Guess isn't my real name?"

He gave her a look that she'd come to know well. It had become a game trying to see how many times she could get him to give her 'the look' every evening.

"You know, most people would say your lack of knowledge means I'm a good listener."

"Nae. They'd say yoo're hidin' somethin'."

"What could I possibly be hiding?" Eesh, could she sound any guiltier?

He squinted his eyes at her, "Murder."

She laughed, it was so ridiculous. "Maybe *you* should put up bells."

He gave her *the look* again.

She lifted her chin. "I am what I am. If it makes you feel better, as potential murder victims go, you're not high on my list."

"It disnae make me feel better."

Chuckling, she tucked her map into her backpack along with the notebook she used as a diary and as a disguise when she was writing to her friends on the magic slates, then climbed to her feet. "I'm going to get ready for bed. I'll warn you if I start feeling particularly murderous before I fall asleep."

"Thanks," he said.

She tottered off into the dark to do her business behind a rock and brush her teeth where she could spit someplace not her tent or with Jay watching her.

"Guess," he said when she unzipped her tent.

She looked back where he was still by the fire. "Yeah?"

He held out something in his hand. "Th' signal's good here. Why don't ye call yer folks. You havnae talked tae them th' whole time I've bin with ye."

As ploys went, his attempt to get her parent's number was sweet but transparent since, for all he knew, she talked to them whenever she transformed. He was a nice guy. He reminded her a little of her dad. Would it be so dangerous to give him one detail about her life?

Best not risk it.

"That's very sweet of you, Jay, but they don't have a number. Sweet dreams and I'll see you in the morning unless you decide to get an early start."

Jay, she was happy to find, was sitting on the same rock in the morning like he'd been there all night. He'd slept though, because his hair was sticking up wildly on the sides as it always did in the morning. Thank goodness she had a beanie to cover her unwashed mop of curls.

"Want a pop-up?" she asked him, pulling a box out of her bag.

"That's nae a proper breakfast."

"But you like them," she teased.

"Fer a wee bite, not a frickin' meal."

"Someone's grumpy."

He turned so that the full force of his glower was aimed at her. "What did ye mean yer parents dornt hae a number? Ah couldnae sleep, thinkin' about it."

"Is that why you were sawing wood all night?"

She was rewarded with *the look*. Grinning, she said, "Exactly what I said. I don't have a number either since I don't have a phone."

He shook his head. "Wa' kind a hippie, doolally pack do ye belong tae?"

"A wee one. You should pack up your stuff before I stash it so it will be easy to carry when you leave."

He opened his mouth, then dropped his head in his hands and shook it again before sticking one hand out at her. "Give a body one ay those."

"I'll give you two."

"Just stash mah tent," he said through the remains of the first pastry. "Ay can pack it up later."

"Okay."

"We're goin' as two-legs today then?" He asked when she tapped her ring against her tent. She was pretending to use it to stash everything because of her company, but really, she was only using it on his stuff. So far she was both impressed and a little concerned that her ring was still working. She thought the magic would have worn out by now. To be safe, she kept a second anchor connected to herself on everything she stashed.

"Yep. It's only about three miles to the ferry, just a quick jog."

"A quick jog, she says," Jay mumbled to himself.

"Come on old man. People have to wait for the ferry. I bet there's food."

"Thaur better be, and coffee."

"Last one there buys," she called behind her as she started jogging.

"Hey! Ah don't have mah shoes tied yet!"

She laughed loud enough he would be sure to hear it, but kept to a slower pace so he could catch up. The morning was beautiful, sunny and not windy for once. Except for the ocean on her left, the land reminded her of Indiana. Okay, Indiana didn't have nearly that many sheep, or roads that narrow without ditches. It did have fields though, and trees.

Jay caught up with her after about 200 meters. There was no one on the road so they jogged side-by-side down the middle.

"I'm going tae miss this," Jay said after a while.

"Miss running down the middle of the road?"

"Miss just running. Havin' naethin' pressin'. Just enjoyin' life."

"It is nice," she agreed.

"It's e'en nicer when ye hae company."

"Yes."

"Ye should go haem an' come back wi' friends. Imagine campfires wi' all of them around ye."

"That would be fun." For a moment she did let herself imagine the guys and maybe Blaze and Frederica around a fire passing around marshmallows. She shook her head to clear the image before she teared up. It wasn't going to happen.

They came to a side road that headed toward the water instead of along it like the one they were on. It wasn't the road to the ferry, but as they passed it, she realized whatever it was she'd been sensing was no longer in front of her. She stopped and jogged backwards. The magic she was feeling was definitely down that road.

"What are ye doin'?" Jay asked behind her. "Did yer forget somethin'?"

She planted herself in the middle of the intersection and stared down the side road. "There's something here."

"That's a holiday park, for folks on holiday."

"No, something magical and old." She sniffed the air. Ocean, trees, grass and sheep, nothing odd, but she knew it was there.

"So we're nae goin' to th' ferry?"

"I just need to see what it is."

She thought he sighed, but she was already too far away to be sure.

The tug wasn't coming from the fields next to the intersection, nor was it coming from the large patch of trees on the right. It wasn't until she could see the parking lot for the holiday park and the narrow beach beyond, that she felt it was time to go left.

Whatever was in the scrubby, yet dense field of trees smelled more like fish than magic, but every hair on her arm was telling her there was something there. She took a few steps off the road, then backed up and untied her shoes.

"We're goin' in thaer?" Jay asked doubtfully behind her. "I don't think puttin' on yer other face will help."

"I'm not going to transform. I don't want to muck up my shoes. You can stay here. There's no point in both of us wading into that. I'll just take a quick look."

"When a hen says tha' it's ne'er quick."

"I'm sure the coffee will still be warm."

"It better be hot or yoo're buyin'"

She set her shoes next to where he was standing on the grass with a flash of a smile, then turned to the swamp. The first couple of steps were only damp and cold, but at the third step, black, dank mud squished up between her toes and by the fifth, her feet were covered in cold, smelly water. She stopped to roll her sweats up above her knees, then trudged forward. The farther she went, the deeper the water and the danker the smell. There was no way a couple of dead fish could smell that bad. Had a whole school gotten trapped and died? She covered her nose and mouth with the collar of her hoodie and tried not to gag.

This was ridiculous. No one would set up a ring of stones in the middle of a swamp. It stank so bad, there was no hope of smelling magic, let alone telling what kind it was.

She should be able to see it though. She glanced back over her shoulder. Jay was barely visible even though she hadn't walked that far. In any event, he wouldn't be able to smell her magic, not with the awful smell of rot everywhere. She switched to her other sight and inspected her surroundings. To her surprise, everything around her faded, including the nasty water, revealing dry land with tall grass and a hill where the center of the lake stood. The swamp was nothing but a thin, painted sheet hanging in front of it. It was all an illusion, even the smell, she hoped. Holding her breath, she reached up with both hands, grabbed the illusion/sheet, and yanked.

Unlike a sheet, the illusion was not covered in dust. It fluttered to the ground and vanished, along with the fishy part of the smell. The rotting part wasn't quite as bad, but it still smelled like something had died.

"Guess! Wha' happened?"

She turned around and was surprised to find Jay right behind her.

"It was an illusion. I must have disturbed it by walking so far in."

"Wow, look at tha'" He nodded past her to the overgrown hill with twelve large stones forming a circle. "That's the' best one we've seen yet."

"Wait!" She thrust her arm out before he could step past her. "I smell magic, and it's not good. Do you smell it?"

He sniffed and wrinkled his nose. "I smell something."

"Yeah. It smells like something died. I think it's a curse. Stay here. I'll check it out."

Jay grabbed her arm. "If there's a curse, why are ye gonnae towards it? Are ye bapit?"

"Nae, I'm…" She lifted her arm although he wouldn't be able to see the hairband under her hoodie sleeve. "I have a protection charm. If this place is cursed, we can't just leave it. People might get hurt now that the illusion is gone."

"A protection charm?"

"Aye. If you're going looking for magic, it pays to be ready for all kinds."

"Do ye trust th' witch tha' sold it to ye?"

"As much as you can trust any witch. Stay here. Curses on a place are usually contained in a border or activate when someone touches something. I don't want it to get you if I activate it."

He squinted at her doubtfully. "How dae ye ken so much abou' curses?"

"Read a book."

She stepped downwind of him and pulled up a shield before switching to her magic sight again and walking around the hill. A black fog appeared, starting at the bottom of the hill. "I think this shallow ditch around the hill might be the border of the curse," she called back to him.

"Maybe we should let a witch look at this."

"They won't be able to do anything but tell us where it is. We can do that."

"Ah cannae tell whaer it is."

"I can."

She lifted her hand so that her palm was flat with the invisible wall she was imagining coming up out of the ditch.

"What are ye doin'?"

"Whatever happens, stay back. If I fall, leave me."

"Wha'…"

She tapped the invisible wall with her index finger. The black fog immediately thickened and spiraled into figures vaguely shaped like armored warriors with swords and spears. She jumped back to avoid the spear one jabbed at her.

"Jay, can you see them?"

"See wha'? Ugh, tha' smell is mingin'."

"I don't know what that means, but I'll agree with you." She stepped forward, then jumped back again to avoid another spear thrust. The warriors weren't following her, which was good, but how was she supposed to get past them?

"Why are ye jumpin' aroond like tha'?"

"It's a death curse. I can see warriors with spears and swords."

"Are ye sure it's nae another illusion? Ay dornt see anything."

"Illusion or not, I don't want to get stabbed. Just stay there. They appear to be stuck inside the border but their weapons can reach past it."

"Wha' are ye goin' tae do?"

"I don't know. Let me think."

It was a blood curse. The vision was clear on that point. Mr. No-Name had likely used the boy's blood to make it, but why did it smell like a necromancy spell? Was it because of the nature of the curse, or did Mr. No-Name have a necromancer friend? Also, who had made the illusion? In the vision Mr. No-Name had spoken like a seer, so he must have called in help after he buried the original curse and set up the second curse.

It didn't matter. The illusion was gone. Her next step was to get past this curse. If it was anything like the one next to Yellowstone, she just needed to put a drop of her blood on the origin of the curse, which was probably the boy's body. If Mr. No-Name was smart, the boy's body was inside the ring of warriors somewhere, likely in the center of the stones.

Getting there was going to be the tricky part.

She tried freezing one of the warrior's first. As she expected, nothing happened. Could she fight them in some way? She picked up a stick and threw it. It went right through the sword the warrior held up, but then shriveled and turned to dust before it hit the ground. Okay, definitely don't touch the swords.

"Why are ye throwin' sticks?" Jay asked.

"Did you see what happened to it?"

"Och aye. It disappeared."

"Because one of the warriors touched it with his sword."

"Guess, this is tae dangerous. We should go."

"I think I know how to break it."

Jay's strong fingers grabbed her upper arm. "Nae. It's nae worth it. I'll call mah coosin. He'll call th' witches. I'll make sure ye still get credit fur th' discovery."

She jerked her arm free. "You don't understand. It's not about the discovery."

He planted his fists on his hips and stared her down. "Ye think ye can tak' on an ancient curse? Is tha' what this is all about? Are ye seekin' a thrill or are ye hopin' tae find treasure like tha' Jones fellow ye told me about?"

"First, he is not real and I still can't believe you haven't seen any of those movies. Second, if there was any other option, I wouldn't be here...any other option that I can live with I should say. This is what I've been looking for. I

178

may someday write a book about the magic of the stones, but that was a cover. If I can get past this curse, I can…," she wanted to say 'go home' but she didn't currently have a home and she certainly couldn't go back to Indiana, not right now. "…I can move on."

"Did somebody put ye up tae this?"

"Fate, God, whatever makes a person who they are. Just stay back, please. I don't want you to get hurt."

"What are ye goin' tae do?"

She picked up a rock, felt its weight, then threw it over the heads of the warriors towards the center of the stone circle. They ignored it. Promising. She transformed one of her nails into a claw and stabbed her hand with it right before she picked up another rock. She squeezed hard enough to get red all over one side of the rock, then threw it to the same place she threw the first one.

"Why dae ay smell blood?'

"Must have been a sharp rock," Honey replied distractedly.

Again, the warriors ignored her stone, but nothing happened after the rock and her blood hit the ground either. Maybe dead center wasn't the right place. Mr. No-Name could have buried the boy anywhere inside the circle.

"Yer bleedin'."

"I'll be fine." She needed to get inside that circle.

"Ay dornt think throwin' bloody rocks is gonnae work."

"I think you're right, unfortunately." She grabbed his elbow and dragged him away. "Come on. I want you by the road and ready to run."

"Ay think we should leave."

"Your thoughts are noted." Once he was standing by the side of the road, she took off her stash ring and handed it to him. "In case something happens to me. You just tap it twice against what you want to stash, and then twice again where you want to unstash it. I don't know how long the magic will work, so keep that in mind."

"Ah could just fling ye over mah shoulder an' run."

"I'd just come back."

She found another stone and bent to pick it up with her right hand while at the same time planting a backup anchor with her left hand on a nearby tree. Was her idea foolish? Possibly. Should she practice it before she tried it? It didn't matter. She'd either survive or she wouldn't. This was it. This was what she'd been searching for and she had to recover what she needed before the world noticed and blocked her access.

"What are ye gonnae dae?"

"Go in the back door." She wiggled her eyebrows at him.

"Yer aff yer heid," he said as if he had suddenly figured her out.

"Hold that thought."

She froze him so he wouldn't get in the way, then jogged back to within stone-throwing range of the circle. Instead of blood, this time she anchored herself to the stone in her right hand before tossing it into the circle.

She'd often wondered if humans could survive in the nether. The lightning bug she'd sent had survived but it hadn't been there long. Well, she'd either survive or not or perhaps be horribly disfigured or come back inside out. She shook her head at herself. She wouldn't come back inside out. Her clothes didn't even get turned inside out.

At least no one would miss her since she was already alone.

She didn't have time for another pity party. Jay was going to thaw soon.

She closed her eyes and prayed for protection, then sent herself into the nether.

18

HONEY – NOVEMBER 7 – NETHER

In the short time she'd known about the nether, she'd pictured it like a big empty space, perhaps with a floor where all the things connected to tethers rested, and then space above the floor where the untethered things floated. She was completely wrong. First of all, the nether had no air. She assumed the liquid she was floating in was water since it was neither cold nor hot and didn't burn like acid, but she wasn't going to taste it to find out. If there was a floor or a ceiling, she couldn't tell, because it was dark, at least to her human eyes.

When she switched to her magic sight, the darkness glowed faintly, like the dark itself was magic. Even darker shadows and shapes floated gently in the magic darkness, but nothing appeared to be moving on its own. Thin filaments, no wider than the finest of spider silk, shot randomly through the liquid, some ending at her fingertips and one at the center of each palm. Anchors. She jerked a pinky and her very full laundry bag was suddenly in her hand. Okay, that worked, but she needed to send herself down an anchor instead of calling something to her, preferably before she ran out of air.

Not wanting to accidentally call the rock or the tree to her, she tried first to send herself to her tent. He tent came to her. At least ten times she sent her things away and tried to send herself to them, but every time, they came back to her. What if she couldn't figure it out? She needed to breathe! What was she doing wrong? The tether was there. All she had to do was follow it. On Earth, it was easy – she just pulled things to her. Here...Oh. Using her things as anchors, she *pushed*.

She landed on her chest, hard, knocking the old air out of her lungs. Fresh air filled her lungs before she could think better of it but thankfully, it was air. Large gray stones were in front of her and, she raised her head, bright blue sky was above. She'd done it. She rested her cheek on the solid ground and let out a long breath. That was dangerous. She was lucky to be alive. She should have thought that through a little more but with Jay there...

Wait, where was Jay and the warriors? Popping into a sitting position in case she needed to move quickly, she scanned the entire circle. The soldiers were gone. Why though? She sniffed. The dead smell was still there, so the curse wasn't broken. What about Jay? She looked all around from her seat in the middle of the stones. She couldn't see him anywhere.

"Jay?"

A crow leaped off a near-by branch, but otherwise nothing responded.

Where had he gone? Had he gotten tired of waiting? Had he decided to explore by himself and gotten too close to the curse line? Maybe he went for coffee or to the bathroom. Yeah, that was probably it.

She followed her nose to the source of the dead smell – a flat rock about two feet square. It was within the circle, but not in the center. Dropping blood on top of the rock did nothing. She flipped it over to expose the dirt below and tried again. Her blood disappeared into the dirt like it had been sucked in instead of merely absorbed. A few seconds later, a white glow bubbled up on top of the dirt, making a thick, iridescent puddle. It kept bubbling up until, like water overflowing a full glass, it started pouring out of the puddle over the surface of the ground around the stones, and toward the ditch. The warriors sprang up out of the ground, facing inward this time, but there was nothing they could do to stop the white from flowing over their shoes and up their legs, and then over their entire bodies before pulling them into the ground.

She waited for something else to happen, for perhaps the essence of Mr. No-Name to spring from the ground the way Mr. Witthem's had, but nothing. Was it really that easy? The air still smelled like death, so she suspected not, but since she wasn't sure what she was supposed to do, she turned her attention to the center of the stone circle where the vision had shown the hybrid curse was buried.

Before Mr. No-Name had killed the boy and shed his blood, he'd applied several drops of his own to the stone box and spoken an incantation. He must have put a second protective curse on top of the soldier curse. With her magical sight and human nose, she inspected the area but couldn't see or smell anything in the location she thought the curse was buried, although it was hard to smell much of anything with the smell of death still lingering. She needed a stronger nose.

She spun in a slow circle and carefully inspected the surrounding woods. No spectators, but more concerning, still no Jay. Where was he? She pushed her worry away. There was nothing she could do about it now. Just in case he was there and she couldn't see him for some reason, she moved so that a stone was between her and the road before transforming to her wolf form. With her wolf nose the ground in the center of the stones smelled like...she sniffed again...smoke. Specifically, the smoke from her parent's bodies and the house they'd burned in, and the smoke of her nightmares when Gaian captured her and when Brayton had burned. She snorted to get the scent out of her nostrils

Was this a nightmare curse? According to what she'd read, nightmare curses made a person's worst thoughts or fears or experiences replay over and over again in their head, making them eventually go crazy. It was a seer's favorite curse. It was also relatively easy to break, according to the memoirs of a curse breaker who'd been alive several hundred years ago. She just had to add a drop of blood and fill her mind with good thoughts until the magic in her blood destroyed the magic in the curse.

No problem. Good thoughts.

She thought of her parents, but that immediately made her think of their deaths. She thought of her friends, but then remembered how much she missed them. Thinking of Brayton didn't help much either. Maybe Jay. Nothing bad had happened while she was with him, although where he was now was worrisome. He'd probably just walked down to the beach. Yep, he was there now, with a coconut and an umbrella, spreading sunblock over his hairy chest. She snorted to herself. What would he say if he could see what she was thinking?

Keeping her silly vision in mind, she started digging with her claws in the center of the circle. A foot or so down, she came to a squarish rock that had to be the lid to the box Mr. No-Name had buried. As soon as she touched it, the dark ideas became more insistent. She pierced her paw and let the blood drip while imagining Jay eating ice cream and getting it all over his beard and his naked, furry chest. He shrieked at the cold and ran into the ocean to wash it off wearing the largest, most ridiculous swim trunks she'd ever seen. A sea monster watched him slyly from the darker part of the water. Honey tried to scream out a warning, but he couldn't hear her. The monster lunged with its mouth full of raft-size teeth wide open. And…no…that was stupid. The water was too shallow for a monster like that, and the ocean was probably colder than the ice cream. Jay took a step back and the monster ended up biting the boulder that was right behind him, breaking off many of its teeth. Whimpering, the monster slid back into the water.

Jay trudged out of the water toward a cheery campfire where Walter and Liam and Luca and Nathan sat on one side. Brayton and his friends were on the other. Everyone was having fun toasting marshmallows and sausages until someone dropped their sausage in the fire. It exploded upward and outward, lighting her friends on fire. She touched the flames and sent them to the nether, but the liquid in the nether wasn't water. It was something flammable. It burst into flame, sucking all the oxygen from the Earth, killing everything, and it was all her fault.

Stop. First of all, if the fire had happened, she wouldn't be thinking right now; she'd be dead. Second, she would have never sent the fire to the nether in the first place. Not only was it impossible, but her first thought would be water or to remove the oxygen. Stupid curse.

How long had she been laying there with her eyes closed? She climbed to her four feet and shook herself. Was she back to reality? All her friends were gone and she was in the center of the stone circle again. That was promising. She sniffed at the hole again. No more smoke. The smell of death was still around though. Concerning, but she still didn't know what to do about it. After checking again so see if anyone was watching, she transformed back into her human form, then reached into the hole.

The stone was cold and felt slightly damp but no visions assaulted her when she touched it. She scratched and dug at the stony soil around the edges of the lid until there was enough room to work her fingers around it and pry it up.

Inside the box were two items: a gold brooch, and beneath it, a rough square of metal with letters pressed into the surface. Sneaky putting something gold on top of the stone. If any criminals got this far, that's exactly what they would go for. Why would a criminal ever bother though? She stuck her nose down close to the box and sniffed. Dust, stone, gold, pain, angst – but which object was cursed, or were both of them? Under her magic sight, the gray metal glowed with a faint reddish hue, but the brooch was just a brooch. Suspicious. Why would Mr. No-Name bury a brooch if it wasn't cursed or attached to a curse?

Staring at it wasn't going to get her the answer. She touched the box and sent it and everything in it to the nether. Okay, one hurdle down. Now all she had to do was figure out how to *seek* for the other pieces and then make a really hot fire to melt everything. Just to be thorough, she sent the box lid to the nether, then filled up the hole that was left.

She did another slow scan, this time to observe the stones and wish again that she had a camera. It would be cool if she could write a book on the magic of stone circles. Oh well, maybe one day when people stopped believing she was cursed. Really, what she needed was a blog or her own YouTube channel. If people could see what she could do, how she could break curses, they would have to believe her. Once again, she needed a camera for that, a magical one that could see what she could see. Did that even exist?

She almost stepped between the stones to leave but a flicker of light caught here eye. Her blood was still glowing in the ditch around the stone circle. If that wasn't odd enough, the smell of death was even stronger. She glanced back to where she thought the boy had been buried. It looked fine. There was nothing coming out of the soil and no magical glowing. Why then was her blood still fighting? Was there a second death curse? She was pretty certain she'd neutralized the curse set with the boy's body which could only mean Mr. No-Name had killed a second person, or he'd buried the first body in two locations, which was extremely disturbing to think about.

"Okay, where are you?" She walked all around the inside of the stones. The smell stayed at about the same intensity all around. It must not be inside the stones then.

With her magical sight, she scoured the ground between the stones and the ditch. Little wisps of something were curling off the ground, but none of them were particularly bright or different from the others.

"Do I want to know what those wisps do?" she asked no one in particular. Where had Jay gone?

She picked up a stick and tossed it onto the ground between the stones and the ditch. The wisps curled around it and pulled it into the ground.

"Death by wisp. Wonderful. Well, either the body is buried under the wisps or it's on the outside of the ditch. I'll think I'll look around the outside first."

She tossed a stone to the outside of the ditch to make sure her trick would work a second time. When nothing happened to it, she anchored herself to a second one, tossed that, then sent herself to the nether again. This time it only took one try to pop back to Earth.

She only had to go half-way around the ditch before she found another burial site. This one wasn't covered with a stone. She knelt beside it and got the immediate impression that whoever was buried there had been young and female and afraid.

Honey stabbed her hand once more, then placed it on the ground and let both her blood and her tears fall. Why had Mr. No-Name been so evil that he would not only curse thousands of people, but he would kill children to do it?

"I'm sorry you were dragged into this," she whispered to the unknown child.

"Stop what you're doing and put your hands up," a male voice demanded behind her.

She glanced over her shoulder. At least four people stood behind her. How had they gotten there without her sensing them? She sniffed. They had no smell. Suspicious.

"Who are you?"

"Enforcers. Get your hands up," the one closest to her demanded, waving what looked like an overly shiny gun. He was dressed in common-day clothes and had a British accent.

"What exactly am I doing wrong?"

"Not listening," he motioned with his gun for her to raise her hands.

With her magic sight, she glanced down at the mound where her hand still rested. A white glow had covered it since she last looked. It was flowing over her hand and up her arm, but also uphill, towards the already glowing ditch. Another person stepped out of the woods, and almost into the ditch. She automatically raised her free hand.

"Stop. Don't step there. Not yet."

Pain blasted her through her shoulder and she suddenly couldn't hold her hand up anymore. Looking down, she saw a hole through the shoulder of her hoodie where there hadn't been one before.

"I wasn't doing anything. Why did you shoot me?"

"You were going to spell him."

She abruptly felt very dizzy. "You told me to put my hands up."

"Why are your hands all dirty?" a woman asked.

"I was, um, digging." Why was it so hard to think?

"Who did you bury?" the man who'd shot her demanded.

"No one. She was here. Mr. No-Name killed her. She..curse..."

Her brain shut off and she slept.

19

HONEY - UNKNOWN

Why was it so bright?

She blinked.

Oh, because there was a light shining in her face. She turned her head, but that wasn't much better. She was surrounded by white and glass and lights everywhere. Even the sheets and the hospital gown she was wearing were white. She wasn't in a hospital though. No hospital would have a room so small with a glass viewing window and no equipment. This was some kind of cell. She switched to her magical sight. The cell was heavily warded, and she, she looked down at her arms for the first time, had been fitted with cuffs attached to the bed. Pretty stones dangled from each cuff, inhibitor stones. She'd never considered it before, but why did Miss Evelstone's family use such pretty stones to make inhibitors?

She started to lift her right arm to rub her hand through her hair, quickly realize that wasn't going to happen, and switched to her left. Her hair didn't feel any longer, nor did it feel any cleaner. She concluded that since her shoulder was still very sore, she must not have been out long. At least someone had cared enough to bandage it. That same someone was undoubtedly monitoring her.

"Hello?"

No response. She wasn't surprised.

Her bed was attached to the wall on her right side. A small table was screwed to the floor just beside it with a white plastic cup on top. A tiny white sink and a white toilet at the other end of the room completed the decorations.

"This is very nice. Very tiny-home modern," she fake-complimented whoever was watching.

The cup was empty, but by climbing out of the bed and shuffling sideways, she could slide her chains along the bar that ran along the bottom of the bed and reach the sink, which she did. The water smelled okay, and she didn't see any magic in the cup, so she drank her fill. Unfortunately, it didn't do anything to ease the hunger in her belly and it didn't do much to quench her thirst either.

"Hi again. I don't know how long you've had me in here, but I'm very hungry. Would it be possible to get something to eat? Thank you."

She plopped back down on the bed. She'd finally been captured. Luna Lynn must be ecstatic.

It was odd the Enforcers thought inhibitors and chains and wards were necessary considering (a) she hadn't done anything to suggest she was dangerous and (b) she could break right through them. She wouldn't though, not until she was sure she had a way out. They probably had a portal blocker in place, but they wouldn't know she had a new skill. All she had to do was anchor herself to someone or something that she knew would go out of the jail and use them to escape or, she could jump to that tree, assuming it was still standing. That would be plan B for now.

What had happened to Jay? Had he been the one to call the Enforcers? She couldn't think of a reason he would. It was more likely that he contacted some witches and they figured out who she was and called the Enforcers.

Her shoulder really hurt. It almost felt like the bullet was still in there. She slowly peeled the bandage away, cringing when she pulled the last layer away from the hole where it had dried. The hole was red and angry looking and leaking blood and pus where she'd pulled off the last bandage. What had that man, who looked oddly like Mac, shot her with? It shouldn't be that bad already.

"Can I get a healer too, or at least some antibiotics?" she called to the air.

They probably preferred her ill and might even hope she died. That would be the easiest solution for everyone.

Three people came down the hallway. Two of them wore bullet proof vests, black military-looking clothing with lots of pockets, and carried long guns. The third, who walked behind them, wore a white doctor's coat. One of the guards, who again looked a lot like Mac, waved a card at the wall next to the glass at the end of her cell. A glass door she hadn't noticed swung open in the wall. The Mac-guard and the doctor stepped inside. The guard trained his gun at her chest.

"Now, you behave and there won't be any trouble," the doctor said.

"Okay."

He looked down at the chart he was holding, then back up at her. He looked familiar too, but she couldn't imagine why. Where had she seen a middle-aged skinny white guy with a biggish nose and straight, lanky hair that went down to his shoulders? A homeless guy maybe? Actually, she'd seen so many different people lately, it wasn't surprising he looked familiar.

"Well?" he asked.

"I'm sorry, did you say something?"

"I asked you what you did with it."

"Did with what?"

"The brooch you stole."

"What brooch?"

"Do you smell it? Do you smell the lie?" the doctor asked the guard that looked like Mac.

The Mac-guard looked right at her and said, "Yes."

"Now wait a second," she protested. "Me asking you to specify what brooch you're talking about is neither a lie nor a truth. It's a question."

"Truth," the man said.

"You got that right at least," she huffed.

"What did you do with Queen Philippa's brooch?" the doctor asked.

"Who's Queen Philippa?"

"Lie," the guard said.

"That was a question!"

"Truth."

Something was wrong here. Why was the doctor asking her questions? Shouldn't that be the Enforcers?

"In case you're wondering why I'm asking the questions, I am also an Enforcer and I do have the authority to administer truth serum if you do not cooperate. I recommend cooperation," the doctor supplied.

And why did he know about the brooch? It was buried in a box for hundreds of years.

"The brooch is a famous piece of jewelry. It was given to Queen Philipa by the king upon the birth of their eldest son. The king commissioned it from one of the most famous jewelers alive at the time. Unfortunately, the plague took him, so he cannot craft another."

The plague. That's why the doctor was so familiar.

"You're Mr. No-Name," she exclaimed. "This is a spell, no, the curse. Oh, I get it. The curse on the box was to get information from my mind so you could craft this reality and the brooch was so you could catch people in a lie. You should have stuck with something simpler."

"That's not my name!" the doctor growled.

"Lie," the guard said.

"This ends now," Honey proclaimed.

"Truth," she heard the guard say just before she transformed her nails into claws and ripped all the magic around her right down the middle.

20

HONEY – NOVEMBER SOMETHING – SCOTLAND

"Guess!"

Honey felt a strange cold spot through the sleeve of her hoodie, almost like someone was touching her with a piece of ice.

"Guess, open yer eyes."

She did, slowly at first, in case it was too bright, but it wasn't. She was back under the trees, near the stones, but the sky had turned from daytime blue to dusk black. Jay was kneeling in the grass next to her.

"Are ye okay?" Jay asked.

"I think so." She pushed herself up, wincing at the pain in her shoulder. She felt the back of it, expecting a hole and perhaps blood, but there was nothing. "Why does my shoulder hurt?"

He pointed behind her where a rock was jutting up out of the soil like a finger.

"A rock, really? It feels like someone shot me."

"Whaur did ye go?" he asked. "Ah waited by th' road fur hours an' ye never showed up."

"For hours? I was only gone two minutes at most. When I got back, you were gone."

"Whaur did ye go?" he asked again.

"I went to the middle of the circle."

"Nae. I checked."

He wasn't lying, at least she didn't smell a lie, but nor did she smell him. With all the camping they'd been doing, that was unusual. "You went in the middle of the circle?"

"Aye."

"When?"

"When ye didne come back."

She sniffed the air more thoroughly. The smell of death was gone. Hopefully so were all the curses. "Just now?" she asked.

He looked up at the sky and frowned. "Nae. The sun was up."

The sun had been up when she started fighting the last curse. How long had it been between her breaking the curse and him waking her? Could she really have been gone for hours when she went to the nether or had she been hidden by an illusion?

"What day is it?"

Jay patted his pockets. "Mah phone isn't here."

"Did you leave it in your tent?"

"Ah dunnae know."

That was weird. He took good care of his phone. He even had a fancy battery with a solar panel he wore on his back while he walked so he could charge his phone at night.

"Where is the ring I gave you?"

He patted he pockets and looked around. "Ah dunnae know. Maybe ah was robbed."

"When? Did you see anyone?"

"Thaur was a wee lassie, but she never got close tae me."

"Maybe you dropped it somewhere. I'll help you look." She rolled to her feet. Her shoulder still hurt, but it was already beginning to feel better. "Where did you walk, or did you walk all around?"

"All around."

"All right. You go around that way and I'll go this."

It was so dark, she doubted she'd be able to see anything, but it was worth trying to find the ring so she didn't have to think of another way to pull his tent from the nether without making him wonder how she'd done it. She was nearly finished with her half of the circle when he called to her.

"Ah found it."

She walked the few feet to where he was looking down at a shiny object lying right next to the ditch. She bent down and picked it up, then smiled up at him, relieved he was okay and everything we starting to feel normal. By the light of the partial moon, his messy hair gave him a very attractive rugged look. That girl at the coffee shop must be blind.

"Do you think anyone would mind if we camped on the beach or should we go inland a bit? I'm pretty sure the curse is gone, but I think I've had enough of this place for one day."

He was frowning, but not in his normal irritated way. He looked confused.

"What's wrong?"

"Aye couldnae pick it up."

"What? The ring?"

"Aye. Mah fingers went right through it."

"Put your hand out."

He did as she asked. She set the ring carefully in his palm, then let go. It fell to the ground taking all her hopes and her heart with it.

"No."

"What?" he asked.

"This is another illusion or another part of the curse. You're not real."

"I'm real."

She looked all around with her magic sight. Everything looked normal, everything but him. He glowed. "Dang it, Jay. Tell me you didn't step over the ditch after I told you not to."

"Ah cannae."

"Do you remember what happened when you did?"

He opened his mouth, then frowned. "Pain, then there was th' lassie. She said tae wait."

"What was she wearing?"

"A frock. It was old with holes and dirty."

"Where did you go then?"

"Ah waited in the circle."

"But you didn't see me?"

"Nae, nae until just now. Why are ye cryin'?" He lifted up a finger to touch her cheek. It felt like someone ran a piece of ice down her skin.

She wanted to shake him, but she was afraid to touch him lest her hands go right through him. "Why didn't you listen to me? I told you there was a curse. I showed you what would happen."

"What has happened tae me?"

"You're dead. I think the girl asked you to wait so you could tell me what happened. Tell me something that only your cousin would know, something you've never told anyone else."

He shook his head. "Nae. You have to tell me something about you. Something real."

She nodded. What if this was another of No-Name's tricks? What could she tell him that was safe? Actually, if she was still stuck in the curse it wouldn't matter what she told him.

"Ah had six toes on each foot when ah was born. They cut them off," he blurted, interrupting her thoughts.

"I wasn't expecting that." Did that mean this was real or did she just have a great imagination?

"Your turn."

"Tell me your cousin's phone number first so I can tell him what happened to you."

"Nope. Your secret first. Something good, like your real name."

"I don't know my real name. I'm not sure my mom ever gave me an official one."

"She had tae call ye something. What did she call ye?"

It wouldn't matter if he knew. If she was dreaming this, he wouldn't really know, and if she wasn't, well, she was going to leave soon anyway. She took a deep breath. No death smell, but plenty of nature smells, including her own funk, but not Jay's. She didn't smell magic either, just a weird clean scent that didn't really smell like anything except it was fresh.

"Why are ye so secretive? What are ye running from?" Jay asked softly. He touched her cheek again. "Did ye know ye glow?"

"What?"

"In the moonlight, ye glow."

Her arm looked normal to her but, "You're glowing too," she told him.

He looked down at himself. "Ah am."

He could see his own glow. Maybe ghosts could see the souls inside of people. Cool, but she would rather have her friend in solid, living form. She reached up and ran her hand over his whiskers the way she'd wanted to do since she'd met him. All she felt was cold.

"I'm sorry this happened to you. It wasn't just some thrill. I'm a curse breaker, the only one in the world that I know of. I'm trying to break the curse that affects every living wolf and witch in the world. A piece of it was hidden here. You helped me find it. If I can do this, hundreds, maybe thousands of future lives will be saved."

"Yoo're tha' hybrid."

"Yes."

"Your parents are dead."

"Yes."

"You're only fifteen."

"You know a lot about me."

He shrugged. "Ah was at the alpha meetin'. Folks is chasing ye."

"Yes."

"That's why ye are alone."

"Yes." Another tear rolled down her cheek.

Being pulled into a hug by a ghost was a lot like plunging into a freezing cold lake but without the wetness. "I'm sorry."

He released her, except for her shoulders and backed away far enough to look into her eyes.

"Now, I've got this voice in mah head tellin' me aye need tae protect ye, and there's only one way ah can think tae dae it."

"A voice?" This had to be an illusion. Why would a ghost be hearing voices? "Does it have a name?"

"Matt. He says tae tell ye he and yer mom are verae proud of you."

"Dad."

The tears she'd been holding back burst out with a huge sob.

Jay wrapped her into his cold embrace again. "Nae lassie. Don't cry. Thaer's no time. Mah cousin is comin'. He'll be here soon. He will hav' felt when ah died."

He tapped her under the chin with his cold finger until she looked up at him, still sniffing.

"Oh, those eyes. Yoo're gonnae make some man very happy one day, but today it will be me. Pull off yer cap for me."

Her hair was probably an awful, greasy mess, but she did as he asked. It was the first time she'd taken it off in front of him. He didn't even look at her hair. He leaned down and placed a cold kiss on the middle of her forehead.

"Ah accept you into mah pack." He kissed her again in the same spot. "And ah accept you as mah Luna." He kissed her forehead on the right. "For now and forever until you find a mate wi' a body."

He finished with a kiss on the left, then stepped back and grinned down at her. "Ah changed tha' last line a bit, but ah think it will work."

The spots where he'd kissed her tingled with cold and something else. Magic? "What did you do?"

"Ah made you mah Luna. Mah cousin will believe ye now."

"But…"

"Ah was supposed tae be the alpha next year. Mah cousin and I take turns."

"But what about the girl in the coffee shop?"

He shook his head. "She'll have tae find someone else."

He leaned down and kissed her forehead again. "And ah have tae go, mo chridhe." He touched her cheek. This time it felt more like the brush of a snowflake than ice. "You are special. Ah was a fool nae tae listen, but ah dunnae regret bein' here wit' ye."

He was fading. Yet another person had died because of her. Her heart, no her entire self, felt like it was crumbling.

"Yer da says he doesn't regret a single minute, mo chridhe," he whispered, then he was gone.

21

HONEY – NOVEMBER 8 – SCOTLAND

It felt so good to be clean.

She rinsed out the third round of shampoo and splashed her face. The space around her eyes was still hot and puffy from all the crying she'd done in the hours since Jay had vanished and Mac had appeared demanding answers. If only she hadn't talked him into one last day.

A fist pounded on the bathroom door so hard she wouldn't have been surprised if the hinges failed.

"Hurry up in thaer! What are ye trying tae dae, drown yerself?"

"You wish!"

Maybe she shouldn't have said that, but Mac was driving her nuts.

"Dornt make me come in thaur."

"I'll tell your wife if you do."

He muttered what sounded like a string of expletives, but he did go away.

She stood under the hot water for another minute, then finally convinced herself turn off the tap. She truly hadn't appreciated hot showers until she'd gone for months without one.

She grabbed one of the white, not-quite-fluffy hotel towels and wrapped herself up, then pulled her duffel bag out of the nether. How weird that it floated in liquid all the time but came back completely dry. She'd have to investigate further, but for now she needed to get dressed. She dug around inside and pulled out the only clean clothes she had left: some running shorts, a bra, and a sleeveless shirt. Well, Mac already knew she was female. Why hide it?

She did wrap the towel around her shoulders before she exited the bathroom. Her hair might be too short to get her shoulders wet, but warmth was a good excuse too.

"Finally," Mac huffed when she stepped into the room. He was pacing in front of the one chair in the room. The other two men were on the end of one of the beds watching TV. "Now will ye tell me what's happened tae mah cousin?"

"He's..." the tears erupted out of her again. Why was this so hard?

"Hey, hey, it's okay."

She wasn't sure which one of the other wolves was holding her, but it felt good to have someone's arms around her. She turned her face into his shoulder and let herself cry.

"Dean!"

"Let 'er calm down Mac."

"Ah want answers!"

"As dae we all," Dean's chest rumbled under her face.

Honey took a deep breath, then pulled back from Dean and wiped her face with the towel. "He's gone," she forced out.

"What dae ye mean, gone?"

206

"Gone. Dead."

Before she ever realized he had moved, Mac was shaking her. "What did ye dae wit' him? How did ye kill him? What did ye dae wi' th' body?"

"Nothing!" She knocked his hands away and backed up so she'd have room to defend herself. "There was a curse. He walked into it. He died instantly. His body turned to ash."

"Liar. Tell me th' truth," Mac demanded, puffing up like a marshmallow in the microwave.

"I am telling you the truth."

"Whaur was this curse?"

"Where you found me."

"Then why arenae ye dead?"

"Because it's gone. Look on Google Maps. There used to be a swamp there. It's gone. It was an illusion that hid a curse and the stone circle. He walked into it."

"Ah dornt believe ye."

"I'm sorry. He was a good man and a good friend." She sank down onto the bed behind her and dabbed at the tears that had started falling again. "Can I sleep now?"

"Nae! Not until ye sae where he is."

"Mac." Dean's shadow fell over her and his body blocked her view of Mac's angry face. "She's tellin' th' truth. Ye can smell it as well as I. Let 'er sleep."

"This isnae over," Mac growled at her over Dean's shoulder.

"I know. Excuse me, I forgot to brush my teeth."

She pushed herself up and slipped behind Dean into the bathroom. It was awkward fitting her tent into the small bathroom, but after some quiet rummaging, she managed to pull out her backpack and send the tent and her pillowcase of dirty clothes back to the nether separately.

Teeth clean, she pulled out her notebook and opened it to Brayton's magic slate. The last time she'd read it, Jay had told her he was going to home. Now he never would.

Somehow, she still had tears.

She filled up another tissue, then looked at the slate. Brayton had written to her twice. She had lost a day somewhere.

[Nov 6, 11pm]
Dear Wasp. Sorry to hear you're going to lose your companion. He sounds like a nice guy. Maybe you should find a place to lay low for a couple of weeks. I could meet up with you for Christmas break.

[Nov. 7, 10:52pm]
Dear Wasp, WOLF was cold today. I have another test on Friday. Wish you were here to help me study. Do anything exciting today?

Dear BB [Nov. 8, 23:03]
Either I'm stuck in an elaborate illusion, or my friend is dead, or both. Are you real? I found what I was looking for. It was protected by a fancy illusion and three or four other curses. I'm not sure how they all worked together, but at least one was a death curse. My friend walked into it. I'm with my friend's cousin now. He doesn't want to believe his cousin is dead, but my friend claimed me as his Luna so his cousin would believe me. I had no idea he was an alpha until that moment. He never mentioned it or tried to force me to do anything. He was really nice. I will miss him. I'm in a hotel at the moment. Nice to finally be clean.

22

HONEY – NOVEMBER 9 – SCOTLAND

She needed to leave. They weren't even ten minutes into the three-hour drive back to Mac's pack and that was already abundantly clear. Could she use a portal from a moving object? She'd never thought to ask.

Mac looked back at her from the front seat. "Did ya hear wha' ah said?"

"Clear as a bell. You called the Enforcers. They'll do an investigation."

"Ya arenae worried?"

"No. If they do their job right they'll verify everything I said. Why didn't you leave me with them?"

Mac frowned at her, then turned forward and stared out the window. The driver, Callen, glanced at her through the rear-view mirror, but again, didn't say anything. He hadn't said anything the whole time she'd been around him, at least not to her.

"Jay marked ye as his. We couldnae just giv' ye up." Dean answered beside her.

Jay's plan did work.

"At least nae until we have proof yer blowin' wind," Mac added.

Mac was never going to like her. That was okay. She was going to leave as soon as she had a chance anyway.

"Are ya warm enough?" Dean asked.

"I'm fine." She lifted her arm to show him her hand hidden inside the over-long sleeves. "Your hoodie is perfectly warm and super soft inside. Thank you for loaning it to me."

"Yeah, he's a big softie," Mac muttered under his breath.

"Jay was mah best friend. It's th' least ah could do for his mate."

Her face burned. She quickly looked out the window so they couldn't see. Mate was such a disturbing word. She should clarify her relationship with Jay, but it was such a weird story. They were already doubting her story about the curse. How would they react if she told them about his ghost?

"When did tha' happen?" Mac asked. "Jay never said a word about th' two of ye gettin' it on."

"Would he have told you something like that?" she asked curiously, fighting and failing to control another surge of heat to her face.

"He would hae said somethin' favorable. Nae what he did say."

Mostly Jay had complained about how much she made him run and how little she talked and how she never wanted to go to a restaurant, both to her face and whenever he called someone. She could only assume he said the same things telepathically. It was no wonder they doubted her.

"It wasn't like that. We were just friends. He only claimed me as his Luna at the end so you would believe me."

"Ye said his body turned to ash," Mac said.

She was going to leave anyway as soon as she found the opportunity and decided where she was going. She might as well tell them.

"It did, but his soul didn't. He said he saw a little girl who told him to wait, so he did. One of the curses got me too, in fact I'm not entirely sure I'm not still in it, but when I figured out how to escape, that's when he appeared to me."

All three of them stared at her. Callen abruptly remembered he was driving. Mac broke the silence.

"Ye think we're doaty, tha' we would believe such naff?"

"I know it sounds weird, but that's what happened. His spirit was there. I know it was his spirit because when he touched me, he felt cold, and he wasn't solid. My dad asked him to protect me, so Jay claimed me as his Luna."

"Yer da'?" Mac asked. "What does he have to dae with thi'?"

"Never mind. I shouldn't have mentioned him. Jay also told me…"

"Why was ye dad thaur? Did he kill him?"

"No, my dad is dead, but I think Jay was talking to him since he was dead too. I didn't see my dad. You see why I'm not sure I'm not still stuck in the curse? The only evidence I have that I'm not is that the smell went away, but that could be because the curse can read my mind and knows it should be gone."

211

"Yer bum's oot the windae. That's th' most boggin mince I've ever heard."

Mac was watching her like she should reply. She shook her head. "I have no idea what you just said. I guess that's evidence too."

"Why didna th' curse kill ye?" Dean asked.

"I got hit by a different curse."

"Why would anyone bother cursin' tha' spot of land?" Dean asked.

"Why do people normally curse things?" she deflected.

"Why did ye get skelp by a different one? Why didna ye just die?" Mac asked. It was clear what he would have preferred.

"Because I could smell where the first curse was. My nose is very sensitive to magic. I warned Jay and told him to stay away but he didn't believe me. I even showed him where it was and what it would do by throwing a stick at it. I don't know what else I could have done."

"Walk away," Mac said.

He was right. She could have. She'd told Jay that other people might die. Really, she'd been worried that the stones would be roped off by the Enforcers and she would never have a chance to get the curse. What she should have done was wait like a sensible person for Jay to leave before she pulled down the illusion.

"I'm sorry. It was my fault. I should have been more patient."

"Wha' dae ye mean?" Mac demanded.

"He was planning to go home. I talked him into one last day. I bribed him with breakfast." She turned to lean her forehead against the glass and watch the trees pass by. "He never got his coffee." She whispered. Maybe she *was* cursed. First her parents, then Brayton, then Jay. Until she broke the curse she was going to have to stay away from everyone.

She was going to start bawling again if she didn't think of something else.

Her next step was to *seek* for the other tablets. From the way the lady in the museum had spoke, she should be able to do that by herself. She just had to figure out how. The Texas library had a book on it, but that would be hard to get to. The Boston library was another option, but also difficult. How else could she get a book? Brayton. He could ask her grandmother and send her the directions. That would work. There were sure to be libraries in the UK too. She just had to find them. That's what she would do then, she'd head for London or one of the other big cities and go from there.

"What's that got tae dae wit' bein' patient?" Dean asked.

It took a moment to remember where the conversation had gone. "If I'd waited for him to leave, I could have dealt with the curse by myself."

"Ye knew there was a curse thaer?" Mac snapped.

"I knew there was something bad there. I could smell it."

"But ye mucked wit' it anyway," he said in disgust.

"Finding magic was the point of my trip. Look, I didn't ask Jay to follow me. I did appreciate his company and his help but I didn't plan on…" she sighed. "It doesn't matter. It's too late now."

Minutes passed. Honey wished she could pull her backpack from the nether and see if Brayton had written anything or even update her map, although the map didn't matter now. She'd finished what she came to do.

"Hav' ye ever been tae a Luna induction ceremony?" Dean asked.

She turned away from the window to look across the car at him. "No. What's that?"

"Well, usually alpha's mark thaer Luna's under a full moon and thaer's a big party."

"Oh." She turned back to the window. "No, I've never been to one."

"We should have one then."

"There's no point. Jay is gone. I'm a pack of one, I think."

"Nae. Jay was our alpha. Tha' makes ye our luna," Dean insisted.

She looked over her shoulder at him. "I thought Mac was your alpha and Fiona was your luna."

"Aye, but Jay was our alpha before and he was gonnae be agin. Once an alpha, always an alpha."

"But you can only have one alpha at a time, right? So, by claiming me into his pack, he started a new one."

"Only until Mac accepts ye into th' pack."

"I don't see that happening."

"Sure it will, at th' Luna induction ceremony in six days, under th' full moon."

Callen was watching her through the rear-view mirror again. Mac was stubbornly facing forward.

"I think I'll pass."

"Nae," Mac said. "It was Jay's last wish if ye are tellin' th' truth."

"I don't want to join your pack though."

"Ye have tae unless ye go back tae yer other pack. Otherwise, you'll go rogue."

"I'll go back to them then."

Mac flipped around and thrust a phone in her face. "Call them. Ye think yer alpha will just accept ye back after ye left withou' askin?"

"He will if I explain."

He shook the phone at her. "Call him."

"I don't know his number."

He retracted the phone from her face and held his finger over it. "Nae a problem. Jus' tell me his name. I'll look it up in th' alpha directory."

She let her curiosity take over. "There's an alpha directory? Does it have every alpha in the world in it?"

"If they're registered."

"What if they aren't?"

He glared at her. "Are ye tellin' me yer from an unregistered pack?"

"Um, I don't know. Am I?"

Callen either snorted or cleared his nose.

"Dae it for Jay's mother," Dean interjected. "She'll be happy he finally found his Luna. Ye can always gae back tae yer old pack if ye dornt like stayin' wi' us."

"But he's gone," she pointed out. "Won't having the ceremony without him there and me hanging around make her even sadder?"

"Nae. She'll be happy," Dean proclaimed. "She's weird tha' way."

23

NOVEMBER 8 – NOVEMBER 11

Dear Wasp [Nov. 8, evening]
What!!!! Why would he claim you as his Luna and then walk into a curse? Are you sure you didn't imagine that? Maybe the curse messed up your mind. You truly found it? Yes, I'm real.

Dear BB [Nov. 9, evening]
He was already a ghost when he claimed me. I think my dad suggested it. I couldn't hear him though since I wasn't dead. I'm pretty sure I found it. Can you ask my grandmother how to use it to seek for the other pieces? If she can't tell you I'll find a library. If I was in an illusion, that's exactly what you'd say, that you're real. I think this may be real though because otherwise I'd be really hungry since water wasn't real in the spell. I could feel pain while I was in the curse, I just interpreted the reason wrong.

Dear Wasp [Nov 9, evening]
Alpha day was today. Dad says you left the pack, so that must be real too. I'll talk to your grandma tomorrow. Are you okay? Did you get hurt? I still have that healing charm.

Dear BB [Nov 10, morning]
I'm okay. I'm with the pack. They didn't turn me over to the Enforcers but the investigation into my friend's death is still ongoing.

I think the alpha is biding his time. Have you ever been to a Luna Induction Ceremony?

Dear Wasp[Nov 10, 1:10pm]
Just spoke to your gma. She's gone to get the instructions. We're at school. No, I haven't been to one. It's usually only done within the pack. The brightness of the moon is supposed to symbolize the purity of the Luna's heart or something like that. Are they having one for you?

BB [Nov 10, 22:45]
Yes. I suspect they are up to something since technically I'm the Luna of a one-person pack. I might have forgotten to tell you. His cousin is the current alpha. My friend and him took turns. They switched every year and it was the cousin's turn.

Dear Wasp[Nov 10, 11:13pm]
Switching every year? That's different. I had to wait until now to copy this for you. It says, 'using a piece of the object or something associated with the object like the hair of a person who slept in the bed you're seeking, attach it to a string. Hold it over a quaerere map. Point down is best if there is a point. Picture what you wish to happen, and when your magic is brimming, speak the word 'invenire'. The piece on the string should be attracted to the correct spot like a magnet to its mate. If nothing happens, you either didn't do it right, the object is gone, the object is shielded, or you didn't use a large enough map. Your grandma says all the libraries have quaerere maps, some charge a user fee.

Dear Wasp[Nov 11, 12:02am]
Dad just called. Mom told someone that you weren't part of our pack anymore, but that you weren't exiled, so now there's an all-

points bulletin being sent out on the alpha channel to report and constrain any wolves who have been accepted into a pack in the last week. Be safe.

24

HONEY – NOVEMBER 11 – SCOTLAND

Honey read Brayton's last message again. How often did Mac check the alpha channel? Should she leave now? She glanced around the room she'd slept in for the past two nights – Jay's room – in his trailer or caravan as the Scots called it. Most of her belongings were already stashed. Her laundry was clean and she'd refilled all her water bottles.

Jay's things were just like he'd left them except less dusty and the clothes that had been scattered about were washed and put away. It didn't feel quite right to be there, but she knew Jay wouldn't mind and Mac had insisted.

Dean had been right about Jay's mother, Iona. She was excited, while at the same time understandably very sad. It wouldn't be right to just leave her, not if there was another way.

Honey packed her slate and her notebook into her backpack, layered on clothes appropriate for both running and the cold weather, brushed her teeth, then stashed her remaining belongings into the nether.

Pulling up a smile, she stepped out the door and nodded at the beautiful blond-headed guard who wasn't her guard for the morning. "Morning, Nora. How's Malcolm this morning?"

Nora gave her a 'I huvnae had mah coffee thanks to mah stupid dog, so dornt talk to me' look.

Grinning for real, Honey asked, "I need to talk to Mac. Think he's up yet?"

Nora's jaw jutted out enough to make hardened criminals in a dark alley think twice about approaching her. If she hadn't gathered that Nora had a soft spot for Jay, she would have tried to lighten Nora's grumpiness with even more cheer, but instead, Honey wiped the smile off her face and gave her a nod.

"I guess I'll find out."

The cries coming from Mac's trailer were loud enough to wake everyone unfortunate enough to live in the surrounding trailers. There was no way he was still asleep.

"Wha' is wrong wit' her?" She heard Mac say through the door.

"Ah told ye, she's teething," Fiona replied, her frustrated voice relaying just how long she'd been trying to sooth her screaming baby.

"Who is it?" The door flew open under Honey's fist and Mac's grumpy face appeared just above it. "You!"

"I need to talk to you."

"I'm busy."

"Bring Skye. Maybe a walk will help."

Before he got two words of his excuse out, Fiona thrust a bundled Skye into his arms and shoved him out the door. "Give me a half-hour. I'll hav' breakfast on when ye git back."

"What dae ye need?" Mac grumbled. His attempt to look mean was destroyed by the caring way he was bouncing his wailing daughter in his arms.

"Where other ears can't hear."

"Finally gonnae to tell me who ye are?"

Her yes earned her a look of disbelief, but he led her resolutely toward the worn path through the open field next to the caravan park. He didn't say another word until they were on the other side of the field. By then, Skye had quieted and was contentedly chewing on his finger.

"Well?"

She tried to feel the tether in the center of her palm that connected her to a tree a safe five miles away to make sure it was still there, but she was pretty sure she only imagined it tingling.

"My name is Honey Smith. I'm the hybrid everyone is searching for, but I'm also a curse breaker. You are in no danger from me because of the curse, but I will go if that is your wish."

In the long pause that followed, Honey couldn't tell if he was just digesting her words or if he was building up for an explosion.

"Ye have proof of this?" He finally asked, calmly.

"Which part?"

"Th' curse."

"I'm alive and I'm not a monster."

He nodded. His nostrils flared as he sucked in a deep breath. "Ye smell like a wolf."

She stirred the molecules around them, making them spiral into the sky.

He scrunched his nose. "And a witch."

She nodded.

"Jay died."

"Not because of the hybrid curse. He didn't know what I was. It only affects people that know, or it would if I wasn't also a curse breaker, which I am."

"And now I know."

She nodded.

"Why are ye telling me now and puttin' mah family in danger?"

It was a good thing Skye was with them or she suspected Mac might try to kill her on the spot. "Because you're about to find out anyway. I didn't want to just leave and hurt Jay's mother more."

"What do ye mean I'm about tae find oot?"

"It's on the news."

"Ye think ye could escape tha' easily?"

She didn't bother voicing an answer.

He turned and started walking back toward the caravan park. "Tell me wha' really happened th' day Jay died."

He was probably hoping she'd follow and make it easier to capture her. She plopped down on the grass instead. "I destroyed the illusion, realized there was a curse, warned Jay, and figured out a way past the outside of the curse to the center where I guessed the origin of the curse was based on a vision a witch showed me."

He stopped when he realized she wasn't following him and lowered his hand to his pocket.

"If you want to hear the whole story, don't touch your phone. I mean you no harm and I feel like you deserve to know the details, but if you try to do anything against me, I'm gone."

"Ye said Jay didnae know what ye are."

"He didn't realize what I was doing, but he did know what I was at the end."

"After he was dead?"

"Yes."

He sank down onto the grass right where he was with his daughter in his lap. "Teel me everything."

She told him about the curses and what she experienced and how she'd finally figured out how to break them. She did not tell him how she jumped to the center and the outside of the circles, and for whatever reason he didn't ask.

"And Jay was there when ye woke up?"

"Yeah. I didn't realize what had happened at first and I don't think he did either."

"What did ye dae wi' th' box ye found?"

"Stashed it."

"What are ye gonnae dae wi' it?"

"Destroy it."

He nodded. "The Enforcers want tae question ye."

"I was surprised they haven't tried yet."

"Ah told them I'd question ye and we could see if th' stories match. Ah used tae be an Enforcer."

"You have a strange way of questioning people. Most alpha's would have tried to use their power on me."

"You're Jay's Luna and you're pitiful with those big eyes always leakin' and shorn hair and skinny wee limbs. I cooldnae dae it. I was hopin' kindness woold make ye trust me."

He considered all the glaring and harrumphing kind?

"Fiona thinks I'm aff mah heid."

"As your wife, I'm sure she knows you better than most," Honey said politely.

He gave her a look almost as good as Jay's, then said apologetically, "Ah dornt see a way out of this."

The three SUVs nearing the entrance to the caravan park started to slow.

"Tell Iona that Jay was and is a wonderful mate," she said, then sent herself to the nether.

25

NOVEMBER 11 – NOVEMBER 15

Dear BB [Nov 11,??]
Thanks for the warning. Got away safely.

Dear Wasp [Nov 11, 9am]
I'm glad you got away. Do you need more portals? I could bring you some for Christmas.

[Nov 11, 22:00]
I doubt I'll stay here that long. There are plenty of libraries and universities, so I should be able to find what I need soon.

Dear Wasp [Nov 11,11:33 pm]
I want to help you find the next piece.

[Nov 12, 21:22]
It's not safe. The last person with me died. I need to do this alone.

[Nov 12, 7:45am]
Dearest Wasp, don't shut everyone out because one person was fool enough to walk into a curse, especially not me because I have a fancy eye that will prevent such foolishness. I want to see what you look like with said eye. Can I please, please, please help you find

something over Christmas break or even just hang out for a while? Maybe I can arrange for your friends to come too.

BB [Nov 13, 6:30]
Don't be ridiculous. There's no way someone wouldn't notice all five of you leaving together.

Wasp [Nov 12, 10:55 pm]
Wow, you are already in tomorrow. Ridiculous! Hah! You should see Luca. I went to the witch fair with him and the guys. He bought this hideous hat with googly eyes because it was on sale. He claimed it reminded him of you. I don't see the resemblance at all. He wore it to WOLF this morning. The eyes bounce down and up with every step he takes. It's the definition of ridiculous. I bought myself a mug that looks like it's pouring off the shelf. I got you something too, but you have to come see me to get it.

Dear BB [Nov 13, 23:11]
I know exactly what hat you're talking about. I barely talked him out of it last year. It's sweet that you two thought of me. I found a store that sells maps. I think it will be safer to trade for them than to seek for things in a library. I don't think I'll be able to just use a piece of the curse, I'll have to use the whole thing. I'm pretty sure Mr. No-Name put yet another curse on it to prevent its destruction. It won't stop me, but I'd rather not break it with people around.

Dear Wasp[Nov 13, 10:16pm]
You are so far ahead of me in time right now, I think I could come see you and hang out for a few hours without anyone being the wiser. Friday is the full moon, so WOLF is in the evening. I don't have any tests. I could leave Thursday after classes and come back

before my first class on Friday. Mom will think I'm sleeping up here and my pack will think I've gone home. What do you think?

BB[Nov 14, 22:13]

I think you need your beauty sleep. It would be nice to see you though. The weather is perfect here and everyone is super friendly, which makes it easier for them to steal things. I saw someone lift a purse off a tourist today. I swiped it back and set it where she could find it. She'll probably lose it again.

Dear Wasp[Nov 14, 10:35 am]

This is your first full moon as a Luna. Don't stand under the moon where anyone else can see you. I'll check this every hour on the hour until you respond. I want to be there.

11 am – here
12 pm – here
1 pm – here
2 pm – your bio-dad just had someone deliver his last two portals. The witch council has forbidden any witches from selling personal portals to wolves, although wolves are more than welcome to use the permanent portals and pay the portal fee the witch council levied.

BB – fine! Realize it's 6 am here. If you come at 7 pm your time you're going to have to stay for 9 hours before it's actually dark here.

Perfect. Where should I meet you.

Sydney opera house. Find a picture in a book. <u>Do not</u> look it up online.

Will do.

And be prepared for a hike. There are some nice parks all around that we can go to. Not sure what the wolf pack situation is though.

Understood. See you soon little Wasp.

26

BRAYTON – NOVEMBER 14 – INDIANA

"What are you grinning like that for?" Cici asked when Brayton rejoined her at the table after putting his magic slate away. "Have a good time with the urinal?"

He wiggled his eyebrows at her.

She made a face and put her palms up between them so she didn't have to look at him. "That…no. I don't want to know."

He walked around the table to take a better look at the sketch book in front of her. "You're getting really good. Maybe you should switch to art."

"Pfft. There's no money in art."

"That's not true. People make art all the time. Just yesterday I saw a new emoji."

She put her arm around the drawing and shifted so her back was to him. "Yes, drawing emojis is a sure way to earn a steady income."

"There is a copy of each one on every phone. Someone has to draw them."

He laughingly dodged the balled-up napkin she threw at him and scooped up his backpack. "I've got to go to the library before class."

"Whose couch are you crashing on tonight?"

"I'm not sure."

"Did you sign up for a room for next semester?"

"I'm looking into getting an apartment off-campus. I saw a roommate wanted ad that was pretty cheap."

"The first roommate left before the semester was over? I'm sure that will go well."

Trust Cici to find the cloud. Brayton left her to her drawing and had to really work to maintain a sedate pace to the library. He was going to see Honey, finally.

"Mr. Mooney, is there something wrong?" a prim voice inquired the moment he stepped across the threshold.

"Not at all Ms. Carrier."

She raised both eyebrows at him. "Then why are you in the library?"

"To look up something for class."

"Really?"

"You make it sound like I've never used the library before."

"Indeed," she said mysteriously and sashayed away.

Weird, unless…was she trying to joke with him?

"Brayton! I was hoping I'd catch you today," a much younger, softer, and flirtier female voice called to him.

"Uh…"

"Janice," the dark-haired girl supplied with a gentle flutter of her eyelashes. "I'm in the freshman WOLF class. You usually pass me on the way to the sophomore class."

"Ah."

"Are you going to be at the full moon run tomorrow night?"

"That's the plan."

"Do you think anyone would mind if I ran with your pack?" she fluttered her eyelashes again.

Should he play nice or just nip it now? "Probably not, but Captain Young usually has a plan. By the way, is there something in your eyes? You keep blinking. There are some bathrooms over there if you need to wash them out."

Instead of being embarrassed that he'd called her out, she laughed. "The other girls said you like to play hard to get. Just so you know, I like a challenge."

"Good for you. I've got to look something up before class so see you around."

"I could help."

"No thank you."

She stepped closer. Whatever scent she was wearing made him want to sneeze. "You know, most guys find it hard to say no to me."

He couldn't hold it. He sneezed. "I'm not interested. Goodbye."

She grabbed his arm. Enough of that. He beamed some of his alpha power at her. "Release my arm and leave me alone."

She released him and backed away with her palms up. "I'm sorry. I don't know what got into me."

And that was a lie. He blinked twice and studied his arm. Yep, another spell. Had she willfully planted the little bug or had someone made her do it? Considering she'd disappeared – he did a full circle to make sure – perhaps she'd done it unwillingly. Had Ms. Carrier had something to do with it? He headed for the bathroom to make sure, yet again, that he was spell free. Whoever was selling those spy things must be making a killing. Ever since the witch council had announced the reward for Honey's capture, he'd been finding them everywhere anyone in his pack went. The eye Mrs. Wixx had given him was really coming in useful.

Finding a book on Australia took a lot longer than it would have to look up the opera house online, but he didn't dare disobey Honey. If she found out, she might never let him visit her again, plus he didn't want to be responsible for someone finding her. To be safe, he didn't take picture with his phone, but he did make a quick sketch on a sticky note just in case he needed a reminder of what it looked like. Hmm, it was probably better to just remember. If he used his sketch as a target, he might end up on a bird's wing or a pine cone.

He checked his watch. It was only 3? What was he going to do for 4 hours? Go to class? Yeah, he should probably do that and maybe shower and brush his teeth. He sniffed his shirt. A fresh one would be wise. Did he have any clean clothes? Shoot.

Class done, body and teeth clean, Rhys' clean shirt on his back, Brayton climbed into his SUV and drove off the campus toward Walmart. If anyone was following him, they'd wonder why he stayed at Walmart all night, but it would be too late for them to do anything about it by the time they realized he wasn't in the store. After buying a few supplies and a smaller, lightweight backpack to carry them in, he headed for the men's restroom. It wasn't quite time, but he could pretend he was a tourist. It would be fine.

"Hey Brayton."

Darn it. It would be rude to just walk by. "Oh, hey, Luca and Walter and Nathan and, where's Liam?"

"He's studying," Nathan said.

Luca sniffed at him. "You smell nice."

"Thanks."

"Got a date?"

"Where's your..." Brayton wiggled his finger up and down over his head to mimic the eyeballs.

"My teacher said my hat was too distracting, so I left it in my room earlier. No imagination that woman."

"Imagine that."

"Have you heard from…" Walter wiggled his eyebrows.

"Zavier? No," Brayton said, nodding at them to stay put, then walking around them as nonchalantly as someone could in the front of Walmart. He found five spells in the first pass, and a sixth hiding under Luca's arm. "But if you don't have anything planned for the rest of the night and feel like hiking, grab some supplies and meet me in the bathroom in fifteen."

He really hoped they had some plans, but at the same time, how could he deny Honey a chance to see her best friends? She'd been alone too long. Plus, it might keep him from doing anything stupid that would screw up his chances with her again.

Luca's eyes went wide. "Really?"

"There will be no sleeping, so if you have a test…"

"Nope. Come on," Luca said, marching with determination toward a random aisle.

"I'll go move my car," Walter said. "I think I might have parked it in a handicap spot."

They all nodded as if Mr. Law-abider would ever, ever do such a thing. It was more likely he was paranoid about leaving his granny car in the middle of the Walmart parking lot overnight.

Brayton spent the next fifteen minutes trying not to look like he was shoplifting the things he'd already purchased. Walter came back after ten minutes sporting two more spy spells. Brayton made a mental note to delouse Walter's car again and destroyed them, then went into the bathroom as soon as he spotted the rest of the Little boys headed his way. A short few minutes later they stepped into the wall of the crowded handicap stall and out into bright Australian sunshine.

"Where are we?" Luca asked, spinning around.

"You don't recognize it," Walter asked.

"I've always wanted to go here," Nathan said, spinning like Luca, but slower, and eyeing the sparse people, specifically the female ones, instead of the buildings.

"Where is she?" Walter asked.

Brayton was wondering the same thing. A woman with long, tangled blond hair, a floppy hat, big sunglasses, and a flowing skirt who was walking along the edge of the cement in front of the opera house briefly glanced their way, then continued on. A light breeze swirled around them and he had to fight to keep the smile off his face. He'd recognize that scent anywhere. Leaving the other three behind, he set off after the woman, taking his time so it wouldn't look like they were together.

"Do you see her?" Luca asked eagerly.

Ahead of them, the woman disappeared around the corner of the opera house.

"Don't you?"

Luca did another complete turn, while still walking in the general direction the rest of them were. Walter shook his head. "Did you guys remember to turn off your phones?"

Brayton had in fact, forgot, but he quickly rectified the problem.

The woman walked along the water for about ten minutes before she entered a train station. She didn't look back the entire time. Had he been wrong? Walter stretched his long legs to walk ahead of everyone and open the door. For a moment, Brayton thought he'd lost her, then he spotted her perusing the ticket options in a vending machine. After a few moments, she tapped the screen and pulled something out of the slot.

"Where are we going?" Luca asked.

"Do you need help," the woman asked with a passable Australian accent.

"Oh, no, we're just…"

Nathan punched him.

Luca glared back and rubbed his arm. The woman grinned and Brayton's stomach did a weird kind of melty, tingly thing. He stepped forward close enough to touch his arm to hers.

"Yes, as a matter of fact. Which ticket do we need to purchase to get to that nice park?"

"Blue Mountains?"

He couldn't see her eyes clearly through the sunglasses, but he was sure they were sparkling with amusement.

"Yes, that's the one."

"How do you want to pay?"

"Ah, um, use this," he handed her his bank card. She nodded, but slipped the card she still had in her hand inside the machine instead.

"Four?" she asked, looking up at him.

This close, her scent was intoxicating. All he wanted to do was pull her into his arms. "Mmm."

"I'll take that as a yes."

"Oh," Luca said behind him. "She's…ow…nice. That's nice of you. Thank you."

"Yes, thank you," Brayton said, purposefully touching her fingers with his when he took the tickets.

"I'm going there too. It's a beautiful day for a hike."

"It is."

"Big place though. Have you ever been?"

He shook his head, unable to take his eyes of the faint outline of hers through the glasses. "No."

"We can go together if you like. I'll make sure you get to where you're going."

He nodded, "Okay."

"Our train should be by in about fifteen minutes."

"Okay."

She tilted her head. "Are you okay? You seem a bit," her accent changed to a Scottish one, "daft in th' 'ead."

Luca laughed. "Nailed him."

"How did you three wind up with this guy?" she asked, leading them toward an empty bench.

Brayton politely let her sit first. He assumed the others would show him some respect since the trip was his idea and it was his portal, but Nathan and Luca immediately plopped down on either side of her and Walter took the end by Luca, leaving no room for him at all.

"We walked into Walmart and there he was," Luca said, "grinning so hard I'm surprised he didn't split his face and smelling good too. He asked me where Delilah was and then told us to meet him in the bathroom."

"Who's Delilah?" Honey asked, wearing her own big grin that Brayton had known the guys would put on her face.

"That's the name he's given to that thing he calls a hat," Walter said in his calm monotone.

All three of them were touching her in some way. Luca was leaning on her shoulder. Nathan had taken a hand, and Walter was reaching around Nathan to touch her knee. This was his date, darn it. He dove in, pulled her up, plopped himself on the bench, then pulled her down on top of him where he promptly put his arms around her waist so she couldn't get away. She didn't relax into him, but she didn't try to get away either.

"You know there are more benches, right?" she said.

"Not with you on it," Nathan said.

Honey turned and tried to look over her shoulder at Brayton. She wasn't very successful with her hat and glasses and wig, but he clearly heard her whispered "Thank you, Brayton."

His chest felt like it would burst from happiness.

"So, why are we here? Do you guys meet up often?" Luca asked.

"No," Brayton answered. "Did you tell them what happened?" he asked Honey.

"No. I don't usually give them any details because they can't see the spy spells like you can."

He gave her a squeeze. She was so thin and bony he barely felt her weight on his legs.

"I did tell them I'd found a piece of the puzzle."

He nodded against her shoulder. "Tonight will be a surprise then."

"Yep," she said uncertainly. He hugged her tighter.

27

BRAYTON – NOVEMBER 15 – AUSTRALIA

Two hours of public transport and another three hours of walking later, they were surrounded by trees.

"How much farther?" Luca yawned.

"Tired already?" Honey chirped. "It's only 3 pm."

"I got up early to study for a test."

"When, exactly, did you accomplish that?" Walter asked, "When your guns were reloading?"

"Maybe."

"Guns?" Honey asked.

"He's gotten himself addicted to a video game," Walter informed her.

"I'm not addicted. I can quit whenever I want."

"You can, but will you ever want to?"

"It's midnight back home. You guys could rest for a while," Brayton suggested.

"I have tents, although this doesn't look like a camping area," Honey said, doing a slow turn to survey the trees.

She'd stashed the blond wig and sunglasses a long time ago, but she was still wearing the long, flowing skirt and the floppy hat. Brayton couldn't decide if it was the clothes, the extremely short haircut, or the thinness of her face, but she looked much older than fifteen.

"Tents, as in plural?" Walter asked.

"Yeah. One was Jay's. His cousin didn't want it."

She'd told them everything, even about him claiming her as a Luna, which made her cry. Nathan was the first one to notice her getting upset and therefore the one who held her until she stopped. Brayton had been both jealous and relieved because he wasn't sure he could have controlled his own tears if he'd been that close.

"Maybe we should rest. We all have class tomorrow," he suggested.

"How often do we get a chance to see Honey though," Luca argued.

"There's not much else to do but wait for the sun to go down," Honey said. "I don't want to walk any farther because I do have to go back for the maps. Why don't you guys rest for a couple of hours while I work on making some charms so I can pay for the maps."

"Do you need more money?" Brayton asked.

She shrugged. "I have enough to last a while. $1000 buys a lot of peanut butter."

"You're not eating enough," Brayton pointed out.

"I'm doing my best," she snapped, then took a deep breath and said more calmly, "It's hard to keep ingredients on hand when you don't have a refrigerator and sometimes there aren't any stores."

"Sorry. I know." He wanted to hug her or at least touch her in some way, but she'd already moved out of his reach.

"Ooo, I want to watch," Luca said. "I watched Frederica make her first ever portal charm by herself. It was exciting."

"When did you see Frederica and did it work?"

"She drops by occasionally," Luca said nonchalantly. "We've become good friends."

"The charm exploded," Nathan said. "She nearly took out a tree. I wouldn't recommend using one of her portal shells anytime soon."

"Hey, it was the first one she tried to do herself. Did you know she has to pass a day-long test and get licensed before she can sell a portal to anyone?"

"Thank the stars," Nathan muttered.

"My charms don't typically explode, so it won't be all that interesting."

"Could you make one that exploded?" Luca asked eagerly.

Honey tapped her lip. "I don't know, I'll have to think about it. I can make shield charms that are reflective so that whatever is thrown at you rebounds on the thrower."

"What if you have two reflective shields facing each other and threw a ball at one, would the ball eventually stop bouncing or would it get faster and faster?" Luca asked, his eyes wide.

No telling what destructive plans were cooking in his wacky little mind. Brayton would have been concerned except it was Luca.

"Depends on how much magic I put into it."

"You could make a perpetual motion machine," Walter commented.

"It would eventually run out of magic, so not perpetual."

"What are you going to use as charms?" Nathan asked.

And so it went. Brayton found a log to sit on and watch them interact. It wasn't exactly how he'd pictured his visit, but it was exactly what Honey needed. He doubted she'd smiled and laughed so much in months.

Near dark, he pulled out the snack food he'd bought at Walmart and made sure Honey got most of it. She ate a bar, made the rest magically disappear, then stood up and shook out her skirt.

"Should we transform?"

"I don't know. Have you guys ever been to a Luna ceremony before?" Brayton asked.

They all shook their heads.

"Are you sure this counts?" Luca asked. "I mean, it's not a normal situation. I've never heard of a dead guy choosing a Luna before."

"Maybe it doesn't," Nathan said.

"I felt the magic when he kissed me," Honey said softly. "I think it does."

Brayton took her hand. "Let's find somewhere we can see the moon. All the signs said there's a big rock this way and to be careful of cliffs, so I'm guessing it's exactly what we want."

To his pleasant surprise, Honey let him lead her up the path. Her thin hand felt both frail and strong in his. The trail opened up after about two-hundred yards and suddenly they were on a large boulder. The moon was just making an appearance on the edge of the horizon.

"Is anything happening?" Honey asked.

"No," Luca said, "except you look odd wearing that hat in the dark."

She took it off and made it vanish. Somewhere to the west, wolves howled, or perhaps it was dingoes. The sound was higher pitched than howls usually were.

"Maybe we should transform," Honey said, turning to him. "At the least, we could have a run together before you have to go back."

He lifted his hand and did something he'd been wanting to do ever since she'd taken off the wig. He rubbed her head. Her short hair was just as soft and fuzzy as he'd imagined it would be.

"My turn," Luca said, rubbing the top of her head vigorously with both hands.

"Hey!" she protested.

"Fuzzy," Walter said as she backed into his waiting hand.

"Guys!"

Nathan grabbed her waist and pulled her closer to him. "I'll save you." With his other hand he gently patted her head. "So soft."

Honey's human form vanished and a small, reddish-wolf popped into existence. She leaped at Nathan, pushing him back a step, then bounced around the rest of them, jumping up and leaving invisible paw prints on their clothes before she scampered away, back down the path they'd come from.

"Hey! No fair," Luca yelled, already kicking off his shoes and tugging at his shirt.

Brayton rushed to strip off his own clothes, not because of her unspoken challenge, but so he could catch up to her before she got into some kind of trouble. There was another pack around. He'd been catching whiffs of them all day.

Honey had a good head start, but the trail she left was easy to follow, until it wasn't. Her scent suddenly vanished. He spent five minutes running in wider and wider circles, getting more and more worried thinking that perhaps the other wolves had snatched her. Then she was there, on the path behind them, in human form with a plastic Walmart bag full of clothes in her hands.

"Hey, look what I found. Can you imagine popping out in the Walmart parking lot in your birthday suits?"

She went wolf again and their clothes vanished. He growled and gave chase along with the other three boys at her mercy. In an open field she was no match for their speed, but in the trees, her small, lithe form gave her an irritating advantage that had him forgetting everything except the chase. It was glorious.

They eventually caught up and circled around the large flat rock she'd decided to sprawl out on, now in human form.

"Looking for these?" she teased, shaking the bag at them.

Walter growled at her.

She laughed. "Don't worry, I rolled up everyone's underthings in the pants they were with so they wouldn't touch other people's underthings. You're welcome."

She tossed a wad of denim at him, then distributed the rest like a queen throwing gold to the masses. Brayton gave her the evil eye while he collected his clothes in his mouth but she was gazing up at the sky where the moon had slowly climbed.

"It really is a pretty moon tonight. Thanks guys for coming to see me. I think this has been the best full moon run ever."

His nose told him she meant what she said, but already, sadness was creeping into her voice.

"I wonder if they have a full moon in heaven. I would guess no since heaven is not a planet, but I bet you can see any moon or planet you want from there."

Nathan lay down on the stone beside her, already dressed except for his shoes, and joined her in watching the sky. "And aliens. Don't forget aliens."

Luca plopped down so his head was next to Honey's but his body was the opposite direction. "Forget aliens. I think it would be neat to go back or forward in time. Do you think you can do that in heaven? Then you can watch how the moon was made, or better, the Big Bang."

Walter sprawled out so that his body was perpendicular to Honey's, but his head was close to hers. "I would guess Heaven follows the same rules of time, but since God created everything and in theory, remembers it, if he shared his memories, it would be like going back in time."

"Rules of time isn't how to think of it," Nathan said. "Time is a dimension. Think of a notebook where every page is a day. You can flip forward or back and since people in Heaven don't usually interact with Earth, there shouldn't be an issue with disrupting the timeline. It would be like watching TV or looking at a picture book."

Brayton tugged on his shoes, then walked around the sprawled bodies until he reached the open space on Honey's left. There wasn't enough room to put his head right next to hers, but there was space near her shoulder. He looked around and sniffed for the other pack one more time before laying back on the hard stone and taking Honey's hand. She didn't pull it away. "If I were in heaven, I'd be concerned with my family," he said, "but it would probably get boring watching them work all day. I wonder if there are jobs in heaven, like guardian angel or planet custodian, or evolution director."

"Evolution director?" Luca asked.

"Yeah, like should these animals grow extra-long necks so they can reach the treetops or extra-long noses."

"I think God has already set up things so evolution doesn't need to be directed," Honey said. "The fittest things survive."

"You're telling me horse manes are necessary for their survival, or human manes?" He reached up and rubbed her head again with his free hand. Her head shifted beneath his hand. When he looked up to see why, the green eyes looking back at him made the butterflies in his stomach take flight.

"Would you find a woman attractive if she didn't have a mane?" she asked.

"You don't have much of one now, and you still look good, but if you didn't have one at all I'd still want to rub your head to see how smooth it was."

"Me too!" Luca piped up.

"You should try that with the next bald-headed woman you meet," Honey quipped. "I'm curious what the outcome would be."

"I bet Mrs. Paulson will let you rub her head," Walter said.

"Ew! She's like sixty," Luca said with disgust.

"Exactly. She's still got a few good years."

"Ew. Ew. Ew. What has living with all those women done to you?"

"Made me appreciate everything my mother has done for me, for one," Walter said seriously.

"Have you decided what you're going to do next year?" Honey asked.

"Yeah. If I can get a scholarship, I'm transferring to Montana next year. I've already sent in my application and talked to some people there. Zavier's thinking about buying a house near the campus so anyone from the pack who wants to go there will have a cheap place to stay. Maya is hinting that she wants to go to college, and I don't see Zavier ever saying no to her."

"Do you think she'll ever say yes to him?" Honey asked, referring to Zavier's open invitation for Maya to become his Luna and wife.

"I think once she gets away from him and sees the world a little, she'll realize what a great guy he is. Actually, I'm pretty sure she already knows, but she's enjoying her freedom."

Brayton couldn't imagine being forced to marry someone and then have their child. He was again glad to be a male.

"Do you guys sense anything different about me?" Honey asked. "I wonder if the Luna mark Jay put on me was only temporary to convince his brother."

"I don't think they can be temporary," Nathan said.

"He was a ghost though, so the rules, if they exist, probably don't apply," Honey said.

Brayton pushed himself up to peer at her face with his magic eye. Three bright spots sparkled on her forehead, the one in the center sparkling the most. He wiped the tear just escaping the corner of her eye away with his thumb. "I can see them. You look like that rapper who had a diamond on his forehead, but you have three and they are much prettier."

"Really? That's the comparison you're going to make?" Nathan snorted.

"There was a rapper with a diamond on his forehead?" Walter asked.

"A pink diamond," Luca informed him. "I saw his picture on a magazine in the grocery store."

The shiniest spot was right where Brayton and his father and grandfather had kissed her to claim her as pack. It should bother him to see someone else's mark on her head, and in a way it did, but the marks seemed fitting, and he couldn't fault the man who'd given them to her when it was only for her protection. He moved his hand up to her forehead. "There's one here," he touched a side one, "and here," he touched the other side one, "and here," he gently tapped the middle one.

She closed her eyes and released a long, soft sigh. If it had been a date and they'd been alone and he'd been more sure of her response, he would have kissed her. Unfortunately for him, none of the three were true, and he shouldn't be looming over her like he was. He shifted back, exposing her face to the moon again.

Luca, who'd sat up to look while Brayton was talking about the rapper, tilted his head. "What did you do? I think I can see the spots now.

"Really?" Walter said right next to Brayton's ear. "Oh! I can see them too."

"They are white, not pink," Nathan said.

"If I open my eyes, am I going to see all of you staring down at my forehead?" Honey asked.

"I'm staring at your eyelashes," Luca said. "I didn't realize they were so long."

Her eyes flew open followed by a glare. "Stop staring!"

"But you're glowing," Nathan said. "You're like a star."

"A fallen star, on a big rock," Luca added.

Brayton got his feet under him, then offered his hand to Honey. "Stand up. I think it's happening."

"What do I do?" she asked, her eyes large. They were starting to glow too.

He backed away, not because he was afraid, but because his intuition was telling him that's what he needed to do. "Just stand there. I don't think you have to do anything. You are a Luna, the mother of your pack. Let the moon recognize you."

"But I'm a pack of one. One doesn't make a pack."

"No. You are the seed of a new pack, the seed that will give rise to a whole new pack, a different kind of pack."

Brayton didn't know where the words had come from, but they felt right.

"She is right. A Luna needs an Alpha," a rough voice said from the darkness under the trees. All around them, naked, dark-skinned people stepped out of the shadows. Aborigines, but also wolves, his nose informed him.

"I am Alpha," the speaker said. "You can be my Luna."

Honey looked from Brayton to the man, then back to Brayton, worry on her still brightening features.

"No. I am an Alpha. If she must have an Alpha, then I am hers," Brayton said. He'd figure out how to tell his father he'd started his own pack later.

"The Luna gets to choose her Alpha. It is her choice. It is the way it has always been and will always be." The man thumped the large stick Brayton hadn't noticed him holding on the ground. "Choose, Luna."

"How?" she asked. She was glowing so brightly now he could barely look at her.

"In the same way you were chosen," the man said. "You are on our lands, under our moon, you should choose me."

"The moon belongs to everyone, and ownership of land is only temporary. Why must I choose?"

"To be a Luna is a gift, one that is not to be wasted. You must choose an Alpha for the magic to work."

"What magic?"

"The magic you feel building around you," the man said. "Choose, quickly, for you will only have one chance."

"I," she looked up like she heard someone talking, and nodded, then looked at Brayton. "Brayton, Jay says you do not have to accept me into your pack for me to choose you as my Alpha. Is that okay?"

"I don't see anyone," Luca said somewhere behind Brayton.

He didn't either but that wasn't going to stop him. "Yes!" Brayton rushed to her side. Whatever magic the other alpha was talking about must be affecting him too, because something was telling him something needed to be done, and quickly.

She took his face in her hands, then stretched up and kissed the center of his forehead. "I accept you as my alpha." She kissed one side, "and I will be your Luna", she kissed the other side, "until you find a wife or your fated mate, or both."

His forehead tingled where her lips had touched his skin, but it was her words that affected him the most. He put his hands on either side of her delicate face, trapping it where it was. "Silly Luna, don't you know I've already found my fated?"

"Who?"

"You."

She looked at him like he'd proclaimed himself the president of the universe or something equally ridiculous. He took advantage of her stunned state to plant a kiss on her soft lips. "You." He kissed her again. "It's been you since I first saw you." Another kiss. "It just took me a while to realize it." One more kiss, then he leaned his forehead against hers. "I can be dense sometimes."

He expected some wisecrack, but all she managed was a strangled, "Huh."

He chuckled, then kissed her again, this time, really kissed her. It took her a couple of moments to respond, but when she did… he forgot where they were. He forgot they had an audience, possibly a dangerous one. All he could think about and feel was her. She was bright, he was bright, the whole world was bright.

"You guys ever going to breath?" someone said far away.

"Tell me when they are done so I don't have to gouge my eyes out," another voice said.

Nathan, Brayton distantly realized.

"You have a lot of room to talk," Walter said.

"I have never kissed someone with that much abandon where anyone could see me."

"You can't really see them, it's too bright," Walter said.

Brayton pulled away. He didn't want to, but Nathan was right, they shouldn't be kissing like this when there were potential enemies about. Honey blinked up at him, surprise, wonder, and dare he hope, affection apparent in her features.

He grabbed her hands. "You feel it too, don't you?"

"Ah, um..."

His kiss had left her speechless. Chuckling to himself, he kissed her cheek. "There's no rush. We don't have to act on it. Just know that I am and will forever be here for you. I am yours, always."

"My Alpha," she said, raising a hand to the cheek that months ago had been nearly burned away.

"My Luna," he said, touching her cheek in return.

"This is like a bad movie," Nathan complained. "Who wrote these lines?"

"Shut up. It's romantic," Luca said.

"Um," Honey stepped away from Brayton and spread her arms to look down at herself. "Something is happening."

Brayton looked down where his chest had started to tingle. "I feel it too."

Honey abruptly popped into her wolf form. The moonlight brightened around her so that she was sitting in a bright beam. A moment later, Brayton was on all fours in his own beam of light.

'*You transformed like me,*' Honey thought at him.

'*And you just spoke telepathically,*' Brayton replied.

'*How is that possible?*'

'*I have no idea. Maybe that other alpha knows.*'

Honey looked around. '*Where did they go?*'

'*I don't know.*' He sniffed the air, but all he could smell was moonlight or maybe it was moon magic. He'd never noticed moonlight having a smell before.

'*See if you can transform back into your clothes.*'

'*How do I do that?*'

She shrugged. '*Just want it.*'

He wanted to be human with clothes. Pop! He was human with clothes. "That is very convenient."

"I know," she said, popping into her clothed human form beside him.

"Could I transform back without clothes if I started with them?"

"First, why would you want to, and second, maybe, but I'm not sure you'll be able to retrieve the clothes at a later time, not without practice."

She wasn't glowing as much anymore.

"Do you think the magic the alpha was talking about is what made me transform like you," he asked.

"I'm sure of it." She sniffed and the corners of her mouth went up. "It smells like a preschool, you know, where kids learn to share. I think it's a spell that allows us to share our magic."

"Is it permanent?"

She tilted her head, then popped back into wolf form, '*Can you still hear me?*'

He popped back into wolf form beside her. '*I can.*'

"Oh, whoa," Luca said.

They both turned to him.

"You've both changed. Brayton, you're nearly white, and Honey *is* white."

'*Well that's going to make it harder to hide,*' Honey sighed in Brayton's head.

'But no one is looking for a white wolf. Mom told them you were reddish-brown.'

"Not to break up the party or anything, but that other alpha said as long as Meeka is watching, we are welcome in his lands," Walter stated solemnly. "Once Meeka leaves, you won't like what will happen. Luna Honey, if you would take care of our clothes for us, we'll transform and then we can all run back."

"Meeka?" Honey asked, popping back into her human form.

"The moon, Luna Honey" Walter explained.

"That sounds like you're calling her your Honey," Luca said, pulling off his shirt.

"Yeah, you're going to have to have people call you either Luna or Luna Smith or Luna Mooney, if you ever change your last name, or simply Honey, but not Luna Honey or Honey Luna. That's just wrong," Nathan said, kicking off his shoes.

"I don't think it's weird. It would work if she joined my pack. She could be Luna Honey of the Honey pack," Walter said, unzipping his jeans.

Honey closed her eyes and tilted her head towards the sky so she didn't accidentally see anything.

"Don't even get me started," Luca said. "I appreciate the reason you chose Honey for your pack name, but there were many other excellent options you could have gone with."

'You're going to have to get used to people undressing in front of you someday,' Brayton sent, knocking a furry shoulder against her hip. *'Especially once you officially join my pack again.'*

"If I live that long."

'*You will*,' he said with a confidence he really wanted to have. '*And I will be joining you once this semester is over. I don't want you to be alone anymore.*'

"We'll see."

NOTES FROM THE AUTHOR

I know, I know, it's another cliff-hanger. Not trying to be evil. I wrote the series with no goals as to how many books I was aiming for, then chopped it into publishable pieces. There are two more pieces after this. They're already written and nearly ready to be published so if they aren't online yet, they should be shortly. Also, the first chapter of the next book at the end of this one ;).

Reader feedback is very much appreciated. Please leave a review if you liked the story and tell your friends and your librarian. (That's me marketing. Impressive, right?)

You may have noticed the 'Clean Fiction' logo at the beginning of the book. I love to read but sometimes, okay often, find myself in the middle of a good story and abruptly I'm in someone's bedroom getting a play-by-play. Sex happens but I don't need to be there. I'm not the only one who feels this way. I discovered whole communities on social media and a magazine devoted to clean reads. To make it easier for like-minded people to find clean books and to encourage other authors to go clean, I thought a logo on said books would be helpful. So, if you are a writer or know one and would like a copy of the logo, drop me a line. LisaL.author@gmail.com. I'd be glad to share. I have both gold-foil and black-ink versions, or you can design your own.

Monster

Curse of the Hybrids

Book 6

LISA LAGALY

 PUBLISHING

1

HONEY – NOVEMBER 15 – AUSTRALIA

"I'll see you at Christmas break, if not sooner," Brayton said, kissing the tip of her nose.

Honey resisted the urge to back away. It wasn't hard. She'd never kissed anyone on the lips before and that kiss Brayton had planted on her under the full moon had been magical, literally. Were all kisses like that or was it just ones you got at a Luna induction ceremony. She kinda wanted to try again.

Nathan released a loud sigh. "Come on, Lover Boy, I calculate it's already 7 am back home. We need to get back to the dorms and take showers and eat breakfast."

"I think it's only 6 am," Walter said.

"Either way, we need to be going."

Brayton clasped both of Honey's hands in his. "You could come with us."

She wanted to, badly but, "I could, but then I'd have to hide in a basement or your cars or something and you'd have to supply me with food and you'd get caught. That won't work."

He huffed out a sad-sounding sigh, "I know."

"And you can't just abandon your family and pack at Christmas. Your mom would be devastated," and she really didn't want Luna Lynn to have another reason to hate her.

"But she's being so...she's impossible. I don't know how Dad stands it. She's organized around-the-clock volunteers to take calls from anyone who thinks they've seen you."

Honey's heart tore a little. Brayton's mom had been so supportive last year, almost like her own mom.

"Does anyone ever call in?"

"All the time. None of them are real sightings though."

"That's good."

She tried to sound upbeat but must have failed because Brayton pulled her into a hug. "Hey. There's nothing you or I can do about it. Mom's stubborn and might hold a grudge against you the rest of her life, but if we can break the curse, she'll have no legal reason to pursue you anymore."

Luca shook his head. "That was the worst pep talk I've ever heard." He grabbed Honey's hand and pulled her into his arms. "Honey, you are nailing this cursed-but-not-cursed thing. Just three more pieces to go. Once you figure out where they are, we'll help you find them. I bet Blaze and the rest of our friends will too. You can stay hidden while we do the dirty work."

"That's a good plan," Walter said, tapping his index fingers on his lips the way he did when he was mulling something over. "Brayton can be the contact point. If you can get us targets by Christmas break, we can divide, retrieve, and maybe portal them to you, then you can break them all at once. Too bad portals are getting harder to come by."

"You guys keep the ones Alpha Silver sent," Honey decided, pulling herself out of Luca's arms. "I've discovered another way."

"Another way?" Nathan asked.

"Yes." She reached up and tapped the top of Walter's forehead with her right pinkie, then tapped Nathan's forehead with her left pinkie, then tapped Luca's forehead with her nose. "You are my anchors. If I'm ever in trouble, I'll try to get to one of you."

"What about me?" Brayton asked.

She wanted to kiss him again, just because, and he certainly seemed to like kissing her but it felt weird to ask him for hugs, let alone a kiss. It would be a good place to set her anchor though.

"Um, kiss me."

"You're going to anchor yourself to my lips?"

"Mmm-hmm."

"With your lips?"

She felt herself turning red again. "I have to touch each of you with a unique part of my body that I don't use to anchor to anything else so I know who I'm going to. I don't plan on kissing anyone else so…"

He cut her off with another kiss so outstanding, she nearly forgot to plant her anchor. It didn't help her oddly weak knees at all when he whispered "That is the sexiest thing anyone has ever said or did to me. You can anchor yourself to my lips any time."

"That gives a whole new meaning to lip-locked," Luca commented.

"Just stop," Nathan said.

259

"Do you have to touch a body? Could it be a thing?" Walter asked.

"It can be a thing," Honey said, latching onto Walter's lifeline and backing out of Brayton's arms, "but if I gave you a rock and then you buried it in a drawer or dropped it in the water or even lost it under your bed, I'm not sure what would happen when I followed the link. If I touch your heads, you should at least be where there's air and hopefully room."

"Does that mean you could pop to us anywhere, even in the shower?" Luca asked.

"Yes, but you don't spend much time in the shower, so that won't be a problem for you," she teased.

"I do spend a lot of time in the bathroom though, especially after tacos. Taco Tuesday. Remember that."

She nodded sincerely. "Believe me, I will."

"Pop to me first," Brayton whispered in her ear. His breath sent shivers down her spine. "I will always be ready for you."

"That's a good line. No wonder alphas are so popular,' Luca said.

"Can we go already," Nathan whined. "I can't be late to my class again."

"Yes," Walter said, pulling Honey into his arms for one of his excellent hugs. "Brayton, I could open the portal to my car. I parked it where I doubt anyone would notice us popping out."

"No. It's infested with spy spells again. I'll send us back to the bathroom."

"What if someone is using it," Luca asked. "Plus, is Walmart even open right now?"

"What about my dorm room. No one should be there," Nathan said.

"But then our cars would still be at Walmart. Brayton, why not the inside of your SUV," Walter suggested.

"I can't see us stepping into it, but we could step out of the passenger door and into the parking lot."

"Yes, that will work," Walter agreed.

"Goodbye, Honey," Nathan said, pulling her into his own hug and planting a kiss on her cheek. "Congratulations on your Lunaness. And thanks for helping me win the bet."

"You didn't win. You bet it would be Christmas!" Luca protested.

"I'm the closest."

"Close only works with horseshoes and hand-grenades," Walter droned.

"What bet?" Honey asked.

"How long it would take for you two to get together," Walter said.

Honey scrunched her nose at them. "Why would you think we'd ever get together?"

The three of them looked at each other and burst into laughter.

"Guys, stop. Walter!" Honey slugged his shoulder.

Walter's laugh calmed to a chuckle and he finally explained, "Brayton has been crushing on you since at least last Christmas, but you were oblivious. It was brilliant."

"I'm glad I could amuse you," she huffed, turning so she wouldn't have to look at them. Could they see her face turning red in the dark? She hoped not.

"Hey," Walter said, putting his arm around her. "We weren't laughing at you, we were laughing at the situation. We love you just the way you are."

"Even with my short hair?" They hadn't really said much about it. She liked it, but she couldn't help wondering what her friends thought.

He rubbed his knuckles vigorously over the top of her head. "Especially with your short hair, but I like it long too."

She hugged Walter back. "You guys are the best."

"Come on!" Nathan said. "We've wasted another fifteen minutes."

"Will you be okay here tonight?" Brayton asked, looking through the trees at the free campground they'd hiked back to after their adventure under the moon.

It *was* rather thickly populated with tents, but maybe that was normal for this time of year in Australia.

"Yeah, I'm sure there's an open spot somewhere and most people are already asleep. They won't even notice me."

He grabbed her hand and pulled her to face him, then lowered his head to kiss her again, long and slow and toe-curling. When he finally finished the kiss, he gave a tiny sigh and pulled her against his warm body, then leaned his head against the top of hers. She couldn't have stopped herself from melting against him if she wanted to.

"Write to me in the morning so I know you're okay."

She nodded. Now that she thought about it, he had been acting strange for a while. Being his (gulp) Luna was going to take some getting used to.